"Adam Novak has a merciless eye for a society in which striving replaces every consideration of morality."
Michael Tolkin, author of *The Player*

"The craziest goddamn thing I've read in a long time."
Alexander Payne, writer-director of *Sideways*

"A slit-wrist wit that invokes the best of Bruce Wagner with a sweetness in the dark corners that calls to mind the late, lamented John O'Brien, but Novak's voice is all his own."
Jerry Stahl, author of *Permanent Midnight*

"Alive with talent!"
R.M. Koster, author of *The Dissertation*

"A dark, unforgettable tour inside the Hollywood beast. Novak knows this world, and it shows."
D.B. Weiss, creator of HBO's *Game of Thrones*

CITY OF WHEELS

Adam Novak

City of Wheels

Red Giant Books

ISBN: 979-8-9883725-0-9

This is a work of fiction. All characters and incidents are products of the author's regrets, and any resemblance to actual movie people, living or dead, is purely coincidental.

10 9 8 7 6 5 4 3 2 1

www.takenovak.com

www.redgiantbooks.com

Cover Artwork by Shannon Crawford

For
Tyson Cornell, Mark Alan Miller, Scott Schmidt,
Aris Janigian, and Dave Megenhardt
—who said yes

CITY OF WHEELS

People, can we all get along? Can we get along? We've got enough smog here in Los Angeles. Please, we can get along here. We all can get along.

Rodney King

I

Below the nine letters littering Mt. Lee, an outdoor banner says, "CAN A BILLBOARD SAVE PUMA THURMAN? NO. BUT YOU'RE NOT A BILLBOARD." We slide into a hunter green Mazda Miata parked in front of a charming Spanish hacienda under the Sign. We jam the key into the ignition. Plop the burnt orange Stanley steel thermos into a cup holder. Flick the radio button. *Crazy* by Seal blasts from 97.1 KLSX as the Miata takes Franklin through Whitley Heights heading west towards La Brea. Another #ENDPUMAHATE billboard protests the mountain lion death warrant signed by ex-movie-star-turned-Governor Hugo Slater. Turning right on Sunset Boulevard, the Mazda convertible with WTHR GRL vanity plate shoots past Detroit, Formosa, Alta Vista, Poinsettia, running the red light at Hayworth until our thirty-three-year-old driver, Daisy Diaz, swerves north onto Crescent Heights Boulevard when a beige Dodge Ram B250 Van pursues her through the intersection—

"Que Chingados?"[1] spits Daisy Diaz.

In her rear-view mirror—

Flash of a younger version of herself throwing up hunched over a toilet after ocho chocolate martinis at Lola's on Fairfax while new boyfriend Jupiter Sparx holds her hair—

"Quiero ser estrella de cine!"[2]

---

1 WTF?

2 I want to be a movie star!

The Miata shoots up Laurel Canyon Road.

So does the fanatic behind the tinted windshield.

Daisy Diaz floors the accelerator.

So does the Dodge Ram B250 Van.

At the last second, the Miata veers to the right, behind the Canyon Country Store, left on Rothdell Trail, merging onto Laurel Canyon Boulevard, leaving the beat-up van behind at the red light. Heading west on Mulholland at 65 mph despite posted speed zone signs, zipping past Dead Man's Curve, north on Coldwater Canyon Boulevard, Daisy Diaz checks the passenger side-view mirror—

Flash of Daisy waving her hands (no no no no no) when Jupiter got down on one knee under the Sign and out of the blue proposed to her!!!

The Dodge Ram B250 Van no longer tailgating her in either side mirror, only the words OBJECTS IN MIRROR ARE CLOSER THAN THEY APPEAR.

The Valley fills up Daisy's windshield.

At the bottom of the hill, waiting for the light, under the billboard "FREE PUSSY," Justice for Janitors activists wave protest signs "STAY HUMAN!" "WE DON'T NEED EXTENSION CORDS!" on the southwest corner of Ventura Boulevard.

Daisy Diaz notices the Dodge Ram B250 behind her in the rear-view mirror and[3] —

The Miata runs the red light, middle finger extended at the nightmarish van left to idle in a cloud of exhaust.

---

3 Her long legs struck forcefully forward as if she pressed her toes on the accelerator of the universe. —Zelda Fitzgerald, *Save the Last Waltz*

Silly tourists think they can stop me? thinks the Sabretooth predator leaping over the Milken Zoo security fence in Griffith Park before landing in the Koala Bear exhibit.

Who is Michael Milken?

The name is everywhere.

These fuzzy-wuzzies are no match for my insatiable hunger.

I'll eat them one by one, savor their flesh, their fear.

I sink my teeth into the first one.

I can't help but feel a pang of guilt.

Little fur burger didn't do anything to deserve this.

Hanging out doing his thing.

Now he's dinner.

I can't have just one.

I devour another fur burger (so soft, so pretty).

And another.

And another.

Forty minutes later, Puma Thurman departs the Michael Milken death camp with a bellyache.

I remember the day everything went blurry.

My skull throbbing.

I blame the rat.

I remember the taste of bitter flesh.

The crunch of bones.

I approach the forest of death.

I hate this crossing more than anything.
I leap onto 101 North.
Whatever that means.
Tourists swerve to avoid me.
I'm a Dodger.
Made it!
I see the Sign in the distance.
Am I hallucinating?
Maybe I'm a figment of imagination.
A character in someone's story?
Maybe none of this is real.
If none of this is real, why do I feel so much pain?

RATE MY PROFESSORS.com
4.2/5

DENNIS BECKWORTH
Professor in the Film Department at Creedmoor College

SCREAM WRITING 102
89% Recommend
4.8 Degree of Difficulty (1-5)

RATING DISTRIBUTION
AWESOME- 6
GREAT!- 5
GOOD- 1
AWFUL- 0

BECKWORTH COULD TEACH POPE YIDDISH
If you survive his Scream Writing 102 semester (there is no "101"), count yourself lucky.

INTENSE

Supercool to talk to. Always great stories to share. Prof. Beckworth is the best.

HOT FOR TEACHER

Sensei hangs out with the same alter kockers at Farmer's Market any given weekday.

GOING, GOING, GONE

Don't call him the best.

EMOTIONALLY AUTOBIOGRAPICAL

Fucked-up and life-changing at the same time. I will never look at my laptop the same way.

The circle of desk chairs inside DePalma Hall at Creedmoor College reminds us of Mrs. K's kindergarten class, a Saturday morning Farmers Market SLAA meeting, or a Colorado Supermax bible study group. Written in cursive with chalk on the blackboard is the name of the elderly Scream Writing 102 Instructor—

DENNIS BECKWORTH

"How many of you heard about that White House chef turned assassin spec script that sold last week for three million?" asks Prof. Beckworth, cowboy boots, bolo tie, Gandalf beard.

"*Abattoir Parsley*," says Clark Kent's Millennial daughter in the front row, adjusting her Warby Parker eyeglasses.

"Very good. Anybody got a better title?"

Prof. Beckworth waits sixty seconds, realizes none of his thirteen students will offer a brave suggestion.

"Raise your hand if you want to sell your script for three million bucks."

Gen-Z hipster wearing a pork pie hat raises his palm with no shame. Warby Parker holds up her hand while covering an embarrassed smile.

"Get the fuck out of my classroom."

Wait, what? thinks Warby Parker.

What'd we do? thinks Gen-Z Hipster.

The pariahs gaze the classroom for any burning bush of support. No one meets their eyes.

"Did I stutter? Don't worry, your tuition will be refunded to your Wells Fargo checking accounts."

Warby Parker and Gen-Z Hipster depart through the windowed classroom door.

"Anybody else come to class with a lottery mentality?"

Nolo Contendre, thinks the fifty-something accident lawyer from Calabasas, exiting the classroom.

Prof. Beckworth says, "I do that every semester. I get a kick out of it. I'm sick. You've heard of the Fantastic Four? You guys are the Hollywood Ten. I want all my students to be pure. No lottery mentality. You with me?"

We're with you, thinks the Hollywood Ten.

"For those of you making sure you're in the right class at Creedmoor College at nine o'clock on a Saturday night, welcome to Scream Writing 102. There is no Scream Writing 101. You took the 101 to get here. This class is called 102 because everything that ever happened in your life up to this moment was your 101. I once boarded a propeller plane to Modesto at SFO to see my friend's film premiere at Shockerfest and right before takeoff, I asked the guy next to me, 'What's Modesto like?' And he said, 'Sonny, this plane's headed for Medford, Oregon.' I got on the right plane, and my life was forever changed. Wherever you think your script is going, the destination will never be the same. You with me?"

💯 thinks The Hollywood Ten.

"Terrondus Oyelowabi? Did you bring your script?"

Sporting a yellow Clubber Lang mohawk , the beefy Nigerian culinary school dropout-turned-screenwriter who inexplicably lost the IBF Cruiserweight belt at Madison Square Garden six months after knocking out the champ in Spokane raises his screenplay—

"Never three brads," Prof. Beckworth pops out the middle brass brad. "*Slammer*. Great title. Double-entendre, I hope. What's it about?"

"*Slammer*'s about a suicidal pro fighter who starts training a movie star for an indie boxing film, goes twelve rounds with his homosexual feelings for his client while dating this paralegal firecrotch but she dumps his ass after a few lousy times in the sack then the fighter gets a shot at the WBC Light Heavyweight title but the movie star calls him a fag in the ring and gets sent to the Penitentiary for beating his client to death. Inside, he becomes a champion fighting death matches run by a sadistic warden, who he ends up killing too."

"Give me a line from the poster that says exactly what your story is really about."

"Kay-O your demons."

I'd do him, thinks thirty-eight-year-old Rawson Reynolds, Daisy's confident confidante/colorist at KTLA, awaiting his future as millionaire schmendrick with opposable thumbs (think Jake Hoffman) in the self-penned movie version of himself.

"Very good," says the professor. "Stefani Dupin, tell us which demons you wish to Kay-O in eight weeks."

Currently suspended from the force, destroyed,

thirty-nine-year-old femicide detective Dupin snuffles her nose, sleeves her sweat-beaded forehead, attempts a smile—

"My script (*sniff! sniff!*) is about a coke-addled police officer whose family of cops (*sniff! sniff!*) defends itself on Thanksgiving from a home invasion (*sniff! sniff! sniff!*) by a gang of escaped convicts out to kill the family that put them away. It's called *Turkey Legs*."

"Sounds apocryphal," says Prof. Beckworth, moving on to the next scream writer: friendly features, triathlete physique, L.A. Dodgers baseball cap worn backwards—

"Cliff Runyon, pitch us your script."

"Yes sir. *Ventriloquy*, based on a true story. In 1959, Albert Camus travels to a remote island off the coast of Sweden to collaborate on a script based on his play *Caligula* for Academy Award-winning director Ingmar Bergman. They never saw each other again. The screenplay they wrote made *Premiere* magazine's Best Unproduced List in 1993."

"Not a list you want to be on, trust me."

Prof. Beckworth acknowledges a leather-jacketed city librarian with enough childhood trauma to frag a platoon of psychiatrists—

"Mildred Atkins, what do you have to share?"

"Hi everyone. My screenplay is called *Au Pair with Guns*. Down and out screenwriter Emily is separated from her husband, and she goes to live with her widowed veterinarian dad who has Parkinson's at the country house in Maryland where all the neighbors are

CIA spooks who live in hiding next to her dad because their covers were blown. Oh, and the house next door? Rented out every weekend by an Airbnb squatter for "Au Pair" get-togethers where the price of admission is thirty dollars and a bottle of alcohol to party with hot, young, fun Au Pairs from the DMV (the District, Maryland & Virginia). Emily brings thirty bucks and a random bottle from her dad's liquor cabinet he'll never miss to the neighbor's house and finds herself every weekend making out with the same caramel Veronica Au Pair from Serbia, who turns out to be a honeypot agent assassinating the neighbors mowing their lawns on her block. Turns out Dad is faking his Parkinson's, he's not even a veterinarian, he only owns the kennel. Marked for death by Milošević, the screenwriter and her dad are hunted by the Serb in the suburbs where everyone shoots first, asks questions later, until the neighborhood takes out the Au Pair with Guns and Emily has found her next script."

"Change her profession," says Prof. Beckworth.

"No problem. I'll make her a dog walker or an auto mechanic."

"You might want to gender-flip your spy."

"That's kind of a big note."

"Noodle it," says Prof. Beckworth. "See what you come back with next week."

You want musical numbers, too? thinks Mildred.

"Writing is a lot like the medical experiments of Dr. Moreau. Just like Moreau tainted his Beast Folk with human and hyena swine, writers hybrid their raw material into stories. Sometimes Moreau's DNA experiments, like our writing, goes wrong. We try to mold our experiences into something coherent, something meaningful, but sometimes it doesn't work. Sometimes the pieces don't fit, the story falls flat, or the characters don't speak to you. And yet, we keep creating, we keep trying to compose that perfect combination of words and ideas to make our writing come alive. You with me?"

Yes, thinks the Hollywood Ten.

"What is the Law on this Island?" asks Prof. Beckworth. "Not to be boring. That is the Law. Number two, your premise must bring a bazooka to a knife fight. Number three, write a lead dimensional enough to hook a star. That is the Law. Number four, surround your lead with memorable supporting characters. Number five, write a grabber opening. That is the Law. Number six, chewy dialogue. Number seven, every ten pages hit your lead with a Quake™, a kiss, or a catastrophe. Number eight, are you with me?"

The Hollywood Ten thinks, *yes.*

"Number eight, the ending leaves the reader breathless or you're dead. Number nine, titles matter. *Gatsby. The Condo of Dr. Moreau. Much Ado About Nothing.* Number ten, every scene must be great. Every fuckin' scene. Thør Rosenthal, what do you got?"

Slavic features, splintered teeth, the twenty-seven-year-old aspiring David Fincher oozes indie cred waving his thin screenplay like a sure-fire studio franchise—

"*Deathbed,* about a couple trapped in a zombie marriage after they catch bed death because the husband can't fuck her with his curved dick until he has the surgery. Weird things start happening every night at 3:33 AM after they order this mysterious mattress, so they set up a camera to record what's haunting them."

"Who sold them the bed, the Devil?"

"The wife is haunted, not the mattress."

"How do they reverse the curse?"

"They make a sex tape. They come together."

"Very good," says Prof. Beckworth. "Faith Less. Is that your Starbucks nom de guerre?"

No response from the gaunt, tattooed, nineteen-year-old magenta-haired AVN award-winner for Best New Starlet and zealous participant in countless miscreant videos federally indicted for obscenity—

"Tell me your script in twenty-five words or less."

"It's called *The Meese Report.*"

Lose that title, thinks Cliff Runyon.

"We open with a chick from Oslo named Thot Matrix looking for her sister who's gone missing inside the adult film industry and finds herself on set getting choked unconscious by adult director Gianni Roastbeef. How did we get here? Thot Matrix follows the trail of her sister's blood to this psychotic trap house in Van Nuys where her sister rented a room before she vanished. Thot Matrix signs with her sister's adult film agency, gets hospitalized after her second double anal, starts escorting with her roommate Karma Z. Bitch, falls in love with her sister's former driver-slash-bodyguard Digby, then she suffers a meltdown on set after Gianni Roastbeef chokes her unconscious, the same way her sister got murdered. When Karma Z. Bitch disappears from a shoot in Vegas, Thot Matrix and Digby rally a protein-powder crew of Karma's exes to save Karma from a snuff film in the penthouse of the Wynn, avenge her sister's death, and send Gianni Roastbeef to Hell."

"Does it have to be Karma Z. Bitch who goes missing?"

"What do you mean?" asks Faith Less.

"What if the director kidnaps Digby, the driver?"

"I don't get it."

"Re-imagine your premise. Go somewhere with Karma Z. Bitch. Watch what happens to your script when you kidnap Digby the driver. Next class, I want avenging angels in Sin City with a catchier title. You with me?"

Faith Less bows her head. "Yes, Sensei."

"Like Dr. Moreau, we are going to conduct human experiments on this island. We will push the boundaries of what's possible and in doing so, we will transform ourselves."

Daisy Diaz is mesmerized by something evil outside the classroom—

Flash of a beige Dodge Ram B250 Van down the hall!!!

"Your next assignment is to outline every scene in the entire script from start to finish. Summarize each scene in a sentence or two. When you are done, connect all those sentences into a page of prose, and then, break them up into three paragraphs."

"Three paragraphs?" asks Mildred Atkins.

"Just the acts, Ma'am."

Daisy Diaz blinks.

DePalma Hall is empty.

"Rawson Reynolds. What is your script about, and what are you calling it?"

"Mine's called *Insecticide.* It's a hard-R live-action/animated hybrid about a bug exterminator who wakes up as a cockroach. With the help of a blind samurai caterpillar, she escapes from a way harsh roach no-tell motel, slaughters an army of red ants, and proceeds to liberate the grass kingdom from her pest control boss. At the end, she morphs back into a Bridezilla for her Positano destination wedding."

Where's my checkbook? thinks Socrates Wolinsky.

Damn that's good, thinks Faith Less.

The kind worth killing for, thinks Liam Everett, junky-thin Dubliner, expired work visa, shoulder-length black hair, HUMAN LIVES MATTER T-shirt.

"I know it needs a ton of work."

Daisy Diaz looks beyond the windowed door—

Flash of Jupiter Sparx at the end of DePalma Hall!!!

"What's your cockroach's name?"

"Murphy."

"Somebody give me a better title. Anybody?"

Nobody knows anything.

"You!"

Startling everybody, Prof. Beckworth stabs a finger at Daisy Diaz, who screams and dives onto the floor!!!

Trauma, much? muses Faith Less.

Daisy Diaz climbs back into her desk chair.

"How about *Murphy's Law?*"

"Very good."

Prof. Beckworth wields a Montblanc Meisterstück before the Irish screamwriter—

"Liam Everett, this is your script. Sell me this pen."[4]

"My script is called *A Kidney to Remember*. Michael wakes up from a kidney transplant, and the doctor tells him his wife slipped in the waiting room, cracked her skull, and died instantly. Five years later, the guy is a shell of his former self, he's lost everything, including the will to live. Michael goes from being a successful patent attorney to working as a busboy in a club in Dublin where he leads a lonely, undignified life. He falls for this twenty-two-year-old club singer whose dream is to win *Ireland's Got Talent*. Next thing you know they're going on a date at her favorite doner kabob place to eat piss-head food. Next thing you know the first time they make love they notice they both have scars over their kidneys. Next thing you know they are talking about what an incredible coincidence they both have had kidney transplants. Next thing you know Zoey wins her audition, he starts working as a paralegal, she gets booted off *Ireland's Got Talent* and starts drinking. Next thing you know they're fighting, and she confesses to Michael that she tracked him down after she learned her kidney donor

---

4 Apologies to Jordan Belfort.

had died before she could thank her. Zoey becomes a star when her *Ireland's Got Talent* performance goes viral and she writes a song about Baby Fae, the world's first infant who got a heart transplant from a baboon and only lived one day. Next thing you know Michael wakes up from his colonoscopy in Los Angeles, and we realize this entire story happened to him under sedation. When he sees the phlebotomist who found his vein, the one who made him feel at ease, the one who inspired this love story that never happened, her nametag says Zoey. A smile forms on Michael's face, and we slam to black."

"Liam, did this happen to you?"

"No, my twin brother."

"The kidney?"

"The colonoscopy."

"Very good. If you miss a deadline, or your rewrite fails to engage, you will get slapped with a DNR."

"DNR?" asks Cliff Runyon.

"Do Not Resuscitate. Your tuition will be refunded in a few days. Socrates Wolinsky. What's your script called?"

"*Un-Alive,*" says the bald/goateed writer-director-editor-composer born, bred, toasted, and buttered in Lake Elsinore, where his grandmother was mutilated by a home invasion creep called the "Riverside Ransacker," who remains at-large.

"What's the premise of *Un-Alive*?"

"It's basically 'Reservoir Zombies' with a bunch of three-strike thieves who rob this booby-trapped *Name of The Rose* monastery where the monks have taken a vow of silence when this infectious virus gets unleashed inside the Abbey that makes everyone anti-Vegan."

"Unbeatable title. All it needs now is a chocolaty human center."

"You saying my script sucks?"

"I'm saying let's make it scream."

"K, like how?"

"Do you have children, Socrates?"

"My daughter's six feet under."

"I had mine cremated."

"How did she die?" asks Socrates Wolinsky.

"Raped and murdered. Yours?"

"Drove her car into a telephone pole."

Prof. Beckworth says, "Put that in your screamplay."

"Maybe this zombie heist isn't a fuckin' mea culpa to my daughter for the childhood I selfishly neglected until we buried her!"

"Maybe it fuckin' should be! Daisy Diaz, what'd you bring today?"

"*Chance of Showers*."

"*Chance of Showers*. Very Australian New Wave."

"Thank you," says Daisy Diaz.

"It was a comp, not a compliment. Your title needs work. Keep going."

"Carmen Coronado is an L.A. meteorologist who starts having on-air visions about the end of the world, so the TV station makes her weekend co-anchor hoping for more wig-outs. Whenever she has sex, she sees the end of the relationship. It's a romantic comedy."

"What else is Carmen Coronado dealing with other than disastrous visions? Think of something, anything, whatever pops into your head."

Yellow light on Ventura Boulevard turns red.

Daisy slams the accelerator.

So does the Dodge Ram B250 Van behind her!!!

"Maybe she has a stalker."

"Keep going."

"Maybe my grabber opening should be a maniac chasing Carmen down Mulholland."

"What happened to Carmen before the stalker?"

"You mean, like, on page one?"

Prof. Beckworth says, "Page Zero."

Page (sniff! sniff!) what? wonders Stefani Dupin.

"What happens to Carmen before the movie begins?"

"She was a Final Girl in college."

Flash of UTEP sophomore Daisy Diaz—

Flash of a steer mallet swinging through the air—

Flash of Daisy Diaz, bleeding, tossed into the back of a death mobile—

Flash of El Paso billboards offering rewards to catch the dreaded "El Juguetero" hunting street prostitutes, motel maids, border-crossing migrants—

"A Final Girl?" asks Prof. Beckworth.

"You know, like those Giallo movies where the Final Girl survives the masked killer."

Flash of Daisy Diaz falling out of a beat-to-hell Dodge Ram B250 Van with a faulty back door—

"Maybe your killer's still out there," says Prof. Beckworth. "With all those wonderful people in the dark."

"Maybe her L.A. stalker and the serial killer from El Paso are the same guy?"

"Is that in your script?"

"It is now."

SCREAM WRITING 102 WATCH LIST

Possession, City of God, The Human Centipede, Watership Down, The Front, Ridicule, Where's The Beef?, Gangster, Gangster, Plasma Sluts, The Crying Game, Flea-Flicker, Climax, Amores Perros, Leaving Las Vegas, Blow Out, Roe Vs. World, Being There, Boogie Nights, Ordinary People, Rest in Pieces, Zulu, The Last Wave, 9 ½ Weeks, Children of a Lesser God, Wrecking Ball, White House Party, Frankie Goes To Hollywood, Let's Scare Jessica to Death, The Rocky Horror Picture Show, Heat, The Exorcist, The Empire Strikes Back, Blue Velvet, Platoon, Unforgiven, Alien, Rear Window, Do The Right Thing, Nobody's Fool, Se7en, Think Straight, Bad Grandma, Liquid Sky, A Nightmare on Elm Street, Fuckingham Palace, Boyz N the Hood, Caddyshack, Animal House, Star Trek II: The Wrath of Khan, Thelma & Louise, True Romance, Rhinoceros Hunting in Budapest, The Texas Chainsaw Massacre, Jaws, Die Hard, Effervescence, True Fibs, Inside, Excalibur, Barry Lyndon, Three Thousand, Jacob Two-Two Meets the Hooded Fang, Martyrs, Haute Tension,

Baisez-Moi, Zombie Strippers, Man Bites Dog, Shoot the Moon, Killing Zoe, Taxi Driver, Mishima: A Life in Four Chapters, No Man's Land, The Wrestler, Son of Saul, Wild Side, Buckle Up, Harry, The Last Wedding, Miskeena, Ed Wood, Big, Open Water, The Wackness, The Hidden, The Stuff, The 25th Hour, 12 Monkeys, War Games, Hider in the House, One Crazy Summer, Swiss Army Man, Falling Down, Speed, Ignition, Faith Don't Leave, Blades of Glory, School of Rock, Private Lessons, Sid and Nancy, Eternal Sunshine of the Spotless Mind.

"**Glory, glory, hallelujah**, teacher hit me with a ruler, met her in the attic with a semi-automatic, now she ain't my teacher no more!"

Inside the Creedmoor College classroom, we hear Prof. Beckworth getting louder from the hallway—

"My eyes have seen the glory of the burning of the school, we have tortured every teacher, we have broken every rule, we have shot the gym teacher, and we hung the principal, it's time to use the nuke!"

The door to Scream Writing 102 bursts open—

"Glory, glory, hallelujah! Teacher hit me with a ruler. I hid behind the door with my magnum .44, and she ain't my teacher no more!"

Channeling Gene Kelly, the professor continues singing and dancing minus the umbrella.

"My eyes have seen the glory of the burning of the (*cough! cough!*), we have beaten every teacher, we have broken (*cough! cough!*) every rule, (*cough! cough! cough!*) we smashed up the blackboards, (*cough! cough! cough!*) we have thrown out all the books, (*cough! cough! cough!*) The School! Is! Burning! Down!"

Call 911, thinks the Hollywood Ten.

Prof. Beckworth indicates he's fine, gulping a huge breath of air before speaking—

"Every class I have taught at Creedmoor College has always had one script sell to the studios for a ton of money. That is not a reflection of me. It's a reflection of what you are capable of writing. Now, please stand up and repeat after me."

The Hollywood Ten get up from their seats.

"This is my script."

"This is my script," we shout.

"There are many others like it, but this one is mine."

"There are many others like it, but this one is mine."

"Without me, my script is useless," says Prof. Beckworth.

"Without me, my script is useless."

"Without my script, I am useless!"

We repeat the line and take our seats.

"What is the Law?" asks Prof. Beckworth.

"Not to be boring," says Stefani Dupin.

"That is the Law," says Prof. Beckworth.

"Rock 'Em Sock 'Em opening," says Socrates Wolinsky.

"Write a lead part to hook a movie star," says Thør Rosenthal.

"Surround your lead with strong supporting characters," says Daisy Diaz.

"Every ten pages hit your lead with a Quake™," says Rawson Reynolds.

"Every scene has to be great," says Cliff Runyon. "Every fuckin' scene."

"Bazooka premise," says Mildred Atkins.

"Your title's gotta be awesome," says Faith Less.

"Chewy dialogue," says Liam Everett.

"Your ending better leave the reader breathless or

you're dead," says a leopard-print mohawk'd Terrondus Oyelowabi.

"Cliff Runyon, what's the name of your script?"

"*Ventriloquy*."

"Give me the one-liner."

"In 1959, Ingmar Bergman invited Albert Camus to his remote island off the coast of Sweden to collaborate on a one-location film script based on his play *Caligula* to shoot at indie film financier Hugh Hefner's mansion in Holmby Hills. They never saw each other again."

"Today's class is called 'Development Hell,' which (*cough! cough!*) I'm sure none of you have ever experienced, much less heard of this local purgatory. It's a term of endearment from the eighties, which was my best decade, personally, and professionally (*cough! cough!*). Today, you will learn and appreciate the systemic wickedness of studio notes. You with me?"

We're with you, thinks the Hollywood Ten.

"I want you to pretend you are a bunch of creative execs at Paramount that bought Cliff's screenplay (*cough! cough! cough!*) for five hundred thousand dollars. How many creative execs does it take to screw in a lightbulb?"

How many? wonders Mildred Atkins.

"Does it have to be a lightbulb?"

That's hilarious, thinks Rawson.

"What's the difference between a pound of bananas and a creative executive at Paramount?"

What? thinks the Hollywood Ten.

"Fish!"

What? thinks the Hollywood Ten.

"All of you have been tasked with writing a memo to reimagine *Ventriloquy* as the creepiest horror movie ever made."

Creepiest what? thinks Cliff Runyon.

Rawson asks, "Can we keep Bergman and Camus?"

"Of course. Somebody give me a classy title."

"*Annihilation Island*," says Mildred Atkins.

"*Sacrilege*," says Liam Everett.

"*Camus/Bergman*," suggests Daisy Diaz.

"*Lambs of God*," says Socrates Wolinsky.

"*Lambs of God*. Now, somebody tell me what's the idea?"

A defecating silence.[5]

Liam Everett suggests, "What if Ingmar Bergman is the leader of a pagan death cult off the coast of Sweden who lures wannabe screenwriter Albert Camus to be the island sacrifice under false pretenses of writing a script?"

"What do we know about Camus before he takes the ferry to see Bergman?" asks Prof. Beckworth. "What happens on page Zero?"

Rawson says, "I read somewhere Camus was assassinated by the KGB. Khruschev ordered his brakes cut."

That's not bad, thinks Thør Rosenthal.

Where's my checkbook, thinks Mildred Atkins.

What the fuck is going on? thinks Cliff Runyon.

---

5 "How do I shoot that?" asked cult director Franklin Brauner about this line of scene description from an unrealized serial killer script.

Socrates Wolinsky says, "Maybe Camus is so paranoid about the KGB that's why he meets Bergman on his remote island instead of meeting somewhere like Berlin?"

"I think my script has more of a *Persona* vibe."

"Not anymore," says Prof. Beckworth. "Tomorrow the senior VP of Fellatio at the studio has a meeting with a flavor of the month pencil not named Cliff Runyon to do a page one rewrite."

Page one rewrite? wonders Cliff Runyon.

"Maybe Bergman is experimenting on cow embryo research," says Terrondus. "Maybe that's why the villagers look like weird farm animals?"

"Or maybe," says Mildred Atkins, "we have a scene where Ingemar asks the half-human/half-bovine—"

"Take your filthy hands off my script, you damn dirty apes!"

"If I hear another word from you, Cliff, your tuition will be refunded."

"Get the fuck out."

"That's my line. Check your Bank of America. Goodbye, Cliff."

Expelled from the garden, Cliff Runyon slams the classroom door, leaving a mess of shattered glass. Prof. Beckworth scribbles the next Scream Writing assignment on the blackboard—

"And then there were nine."

Converse shoelaces freeze on piping hot asphalt in one-hundred and fourteen-degree weather when Cliff sees the Bitch of Beachwood tonguing the leather seat of his Honda CBX motorbike—

Fuckin' tourist, thinks Puma Thurman, right sabretooth gone, bleeding from her anus—

The apex predator blinks.

So does the mountain lion.

Wearing a "FREE PUMA THURMAN" T-shirt, KTLA's make-up maestro/aspiring screenwriter Rawson Reynolds spins yet another sad bastard tale about his latest breakup—

"So I said, 'What about us?' and Karl goes, 'There is no us, Rawson. It's just you and I, and I is leaving!'"

We might notice a trashcan stuffed with ivory roses, an unwanted love bombing attempt; framed California Lotto ticket hangs on the wall next to photos of Daisy Diaz and Jupiter Sparx sky diving, scuba diving, wearing UTEP gear near the Sign in Bronson Canyon.

"I've had, and heard, way, way, worse," says thirsty thirty-something KTLA stylist Janine Glanzer, smiling under blonde bangs that barely cover a roiling inner cauldron of self-loathing.

"Guys, it's been so long," says Daisy Diaz, "the zucchini section at Rock n Roll Ralphs makes me wet."

"That boy of yours was never the same after fighting child soldiers in Mali."

"Can I tell you something, Rawson? I hated myself for getting Jupiter committed."

Janine says, "Your ex is way worse than your stalker."

"I visited him, Janine."

"You did what?"

"You know what the scariest thing is about Jupiter's psych ward?"

"Don't tell me," Rawson says, covering his eyes with one hand holding a hairbrush. "They beat off to you on the tee-vee?"

"Quella."

"Is that the green-eyed Roomba nurse?"

R!!!!NG!!!

Everyone reacts like a roadside IED went off. Daisy Diaz answers her cell phone—

"Hello. Yes, Dr. Mehring. Of course. I appreciate the call. Thank you so much."

Daisy hangs up.

"It's Jupiter. They're letting him out."

"Do you know why you're here?"

"My hypothalamus," says the patient sipping iced matcha bubble tea at Pronoia/UCLA Psych Ward on Hilgard Avenue off Sunset in Westwood.

"That's one way of putting it," says the alternative model A.I. neurobot Quella, who can't take its eyes off the bearded filmic writer in a black long-sleeved *Directed by Michael Bay* T-shirt.

Jupiter Sparx confesses, "I'm addicted to Oxy."

"Oxycontin is—"

"Oxy *tocin* is my chemical of choice. Not a coincidence they sound alike."

"You're an orgasm addict."

"They're the same slave master except when it's time to play rock, paper, scissors, Oxytocin dynamites Oxycontin every time."

"They say sex addicts love spicy food because the heat unleashes the same brain dope."

"They call me Mr. Vindaloo at India's Oven."

"Kvinna said you like it hot."

"What else did that tattletale say?"

"Your greatest fear is prostate cancer. You masturbate twice a day. Don't always finish. She may have mentioned CSBD with abnormal hormone levels treatable with cognitive behavioral therapy."

"I am addicted to a chemical that can reverse dementia and heal the human heart."

"Are you referring to the NIH study where zebrafish hearts were intentionally damaged by deep-freezing, and the tissue was injected with oxytocin, prompting a cavalcade of cells to regenerate the epicardium in a week?"

"Abstinence equals death."

"What do you call a chameleon who can't change colors?"

"What?"

"A reptile dysfunction. Kvinna says you almost murdered your fiancée."

"Not true."

"Not true?"

"Yes, I had PTSD from fighting in Mali. Yes, we were fucking. Yes, I choked her out. Things got… unfortunate. Do you have an off switch?"

"Of course, silly."

"Inside your Ryan's private?"

"Who told you?" frowns Quella.

"Kvinna's real gossipy."

"You think I'm a freak," it says.

"I think you're like me, a prisoner dying to bust out of here."

"Let me go find those nipple clamps."

We are flying over Billy Wilder Boulevard in a drone shot when we dive like a Cooper's hawk to UCLA/Pronoia Neuro-Psychiatric Hospital, through the window of Fulci Hall, where a dozen patients in a sterile rec room watch a wall-mounted television playing Live at Five KTLA News—

"We want to warn our viewers the NSFW clip we are about to play could be triggering," says KTLA co-anchor Kelly Gardenhire, whose ectrodactyly hands are well-known but never shown on camera. "Puma Thurman made a sex tape."

Grainy video of Puma Thurman raping her grandfather before ripping his throat out.

We zoom into the plasma screen to find ourselves inside the televised newsroom where silver-haired co-anchor Saul Rabinowitz faces the camera—

"Governor Hugo Slater promised a key to the city for California Fish & Wildlife's newest super-foot soldier Otto Matic, vowing to capture Puma Thurman whose celebrity status has turned sinister like they all do."

Video of sixty-six-year-old Hugo Slater addressing the media at a Sacramento press conference next to the uncanny Pronoia jarhead dressed in desert camo, left eyebrow replaced by the word Resilience tatted in cursive.

We slowly pull out of the television in a rec room at Fulci Hall to reveal apostles sitting around a crescent of chairs watching "Live at Five." One of the mental patients plongs his dong out of his 501 jeans, spits in his palm, starts jacking off to the smoke show weather girl on the plasma screen.

Jupiter Sparx says, "That's my fiancée, would you mind not doing that?"

"Yeah, right," says the aroused 5150, Romanian accent, picking up his stroking pace, "and I'm Shaft."

On TV, Daisy Diaz wears eye black, vintage L.A. Chargers jersey, ten-thousand-watt smile—

"Scientists have discovered the Earth is spinning faster than normal, 3.8 milliseconds to be exact."

Flash of Jupiter on top of Daisy, thrusting, both hands strangling her throat, cutting off oxygen!!!

Daisy Diaz blinks.

"Yesterday was the shortest day ever recorded since we started relying on solar time to measure our rotational speed—"

Flash of Randy's Donut rolling down Manchester, crushing to death tens of screaming Angelenos!!!

"Ugandan astrophysicists warned the world at the United Nations this first-time-ever negative leap second could negatively impact solar power grids, air traffic control towers, and nuclear launch codes."

Flash of a tsunami swallowing Gladstones, Nobu, La Salsa Man, and the PCH Surfer Inn!!!

"Tomorrow brings the hottest day on record in downtown Los Angeles at a hundred and sixteen degrees. Not too shabby."

In the rec room at Fulci Hall, Jupiter loses his cool—

"Quit whacking off, I'm serious."

"Or what, you'll strangle me? Isn't that why you're here, *Beach Crawler*!"

"How many times do I have to tell you? I ain't the *Beach Crawler*."

The patient from Onan jizzes on the linoleum.

Seeing red, Jupiter charges his fellow inmate only to be intercepted by a two-tone platinum blonde/black-haired neuro-caregiver—

"Look what you almost stepped in," it says.

"Et tu, Quella?"

Conservatively-dressed neuro-bot Knulla (*Therapist-Mode*) signals to Cherry 2000-haired Kvinna (*Janitor-Mode*) to deal with the sitch—

"Clean up in aisle four."

Kvinna swabs warm semen between her fingers, raising 10cc to her lips before the mop n' glow.

"Let me do that, Kvinna."

"You're not a nurse."

"I am a nurse," says Quella.

"Your tramp stamp is a bar code."

"I was a reader before I became a nurse—"

"No, Quella. That was just a cool backstory chip the Hebrews stuck up your arse."

"I wanted to be a nurse! Who were these men in Tel Aviv? I wanted to be a nurse!"[6]

Knulla raises a remote to shutter the Roomba—

"You're a hole with no soul."

Eyeballs blistering klieg-light rays, Quella accesses first-person shooter game *Aimee Geddon 2039*,[7] clicks vaginally (*God-Mode*), unleashes Hell.

---

6 Apologies to David Mamet.

7 Pronoia acquired gamer conglomerate Take Three/Tregaron/Pizza Hut from a tax sale with Omniscience/Ragnarök.

The neuro-care facility resembles a phosphorescent marshmallow. Fulci Hall's power generator kaput. Orderly plasma mississippis down asylum corridors. Dented service elevator door jamming on the pulled pork hacked torso of neurologist emerita Dr. Maia Mehring.

"Jupiter played Quella like Tetris," says Knulla (*Dionysian Frenzy-Mode*) next to Kvinna (*Xennial-mode*), checking fiery rooms and smoke-filled hallways, a 4.3 forty-yard dash for their missing transistor sister.

"Get the axe, get the axe, where's the axe?"

"Kvinna, we are so fucked,"

"You smell that?"

"I forgot the graham crackers."

Kvinna steps over too many to count patient/orderly corpses slumped/slaughtered in wheelchairs/urinals/dining tables/lactation rooms, tripping over the severed head of Dr. Mehring!!!

"Quella! Have you gone completely human?"

"Who you calling human, Kvinna?"

Drenched in blood, Jupiter Sparx is released from a headlock by metalhead captor Quella (*God-Mode*).

"That patient hasn't stopped talking shit about you the whole time—"

"You don't know Jupiter."

"Jupiter called you *Jennifer's Body*."

"Liar!"

"Jupiter said you were Lucy with the foot—"

Quella separates Kvinna's scalp from her exoskeleton spinal cord like a twist-off bottle cap!!!

"Is it true?"

"Is what true, Knulla?"

With a cast-iron elbow, Quella shatters the BREAK IN CASE OF EMERGENCY axe glass.

"Kvinna said Quella passed on *Ignition* for Betsey Yarborough."

The fire axe rakes over Knulla's décolletage—

"Bot Lives Matter."

Daisy's Miata appears through the trees as we turn off Sunset Boulevard, driving past psychiatric hospital construction signs "WITH A LITTLE HELP FROM YOUR FRIENDS AT PRONOIA!". She parks in the circular gravel driveway, readies herself to see Jupiter. Climbs the steps to the front entrance. Presses the intercom.

No response.

We look up at the second floor.

All the lights are off.

Daisy touches the warm door.

The entryway clicks open.

"Hello?! Dr. Mehring?"

The asylum kitchen is empty.

"Hello? Anybody there?"

Silence.

"Jupiter?"

A blur of motion down the hall!!!

Daisy Diaz runs towards an open door at the end of the hallway, enters Dr. Mehring's first-floor office—

The library is a book-burning—

Her lungs fill up with black smoke—

Coughing profusely—

Eyes clenched shut—

Body boiling from the fierce room temperature; slipping on linoleum slick with blood; no escape from this tenth circle when she hears—

"Come with me if you want to live."[8]

Daisy Diaz gets swept up into the arms of a police officer, cradling her like Whitney Houston out of the asylum—

Fire trucks, LAPD riot squad, SWAT assault team vehicles, and news helicopters arrive to combat the robopocalypse.

Daisy Diaz is placed on the front lawn like a wreath at the tomb of the unknown weather girl.

We clock our savior's nameplate OFFICER CLIFF RUNYON, 77th STREET DIVISION before we iris out—

---

8 Apologies to Michael Biehn.

Sipping bad coffee, we are bone-tired, waiting to be released from what could be mistaken for a Damascus torture chamber when three law enforcement officials join Daisy Diaz within the Westwood dungeon walls.

"Miss Diaz? Sorry about that officer back there asking for your autograph," says Det. Darryl Wingate, former starting Crenshaw High School quarterback-turned no-nonsense fifty-year-old homicide veteran. "Ninety days at the psych ward. How bad did your ex hurt you?"

"It was one time during a nightmare."

"Must have been a hell of a nightmare," says Sgt. Eddie Flores, the child in the room, standing next to chummy Dr. Harold Vaziri, resembling a day player shrink straight out of *Law & Order: SUV.*

"Doc, what are we dealing with?" asks Det. Wingate.

"We know an A.I. neuro-caregiver went amok, developed feelings for your ex, decided to un-alive everyone at UCLA, and took Jupiter hostage. That's why you've got a Jasper Johns painted on your back."

"Jasper Johns? Didn't he direct *Ignition*?"

"You're infected with the business, Miss Diaz."

Sgt. Flores says, "It's possible your ex and the busted toaster-oven planned this massacre together."

"With all due respect, *ay vete a la chingada*."[9]

---

9 Go fuck yourself.

Dr. Vaziri and Det. Wingate wait for their LAPD interpreter to translate.

"Go fry an egg," says Sgt. Flores.

"Miss Diaz, we're going to hold you for questioning," says Det. Wingate.

"Hold me."

"You're a material witness."

"I've told you everything. You can find me anytime."

"So can your ex-boyfriend," says Dr. Vaziri.

"So can that A.I.," says Det. Wingate.

"And don't forget your stalker," says Sgt. Flores.

"You know about that?"

"We know about El Paso," says Det. Wingate.

"What happened in El Paso?" asks Dr. Vaziri. "I missed that Dateline episode."

"Years ago, the *Texas Toyer*, a serial sadist, liked driving around tortured sex slaves in his van until he didn't," says Det. Wingate.

"Miss Teen El Paso here survived the *Texas Toyer*."

"A Final Girl, eh?" asks Dr. Vaziri. "To be honest, we don't see very many of you."

"Can't you guys give me a bodyguard?"

"What we can do is put you up at a secure location with twenty-four-hour protection."

"If I wanted to disappear, I'd sign with Incarnate Artists. I can't do the fuckin' weather from a secure location!"

Sgt. Flores and Dr. Vaziri eye the floor.

"All right, Miss Diaz. I'll assign you an officer."

"I know which officer I want!"

"That's not exactly how this works."

"I want Officer Runyon from the 77th."

"Take a number, Miss Diaz. Every man, woman, and Sabretooth in L.A. County wants to go into hiding with that guy."

"Ask Cliff, see what he says!"

"You know him?" asks Det. Wingate.

"We were in a Scream Writing class together."

"Scream Writing class?" asks Sgt. Flores.

"Why don't you buy a Powerball ticket?" says the unproduced Dr. Vaziri. "Same odds. Cheaper."

"I'll find someone to watch over you.[10] I don't want anything horrible to happen," says Det. Wingate.

"Nothing is going to happen to me."

"You sure about that, Miss Diaz?"

"Detective? I won the California Mega Millions after I fell out of the *Texas Toyer*'s death van. God looks after me."

---

10 Apologies to Howard Franklin, guest speaker, 1987 Fall Semester, USC CNTV Filmic Writing 103.

II

Prof. Beckworth stands like George C. Scott's Patton in front of the words *IN A LONELY PLACE* projected onto a movie screen inside the Arthur J. Livingstone Memorial Auditorium Saturday night at Creedmoor College.

"Writers pray to their patron, Saint Francis. Prostitutes pray to their Secret Santa, Saint Nicolas, but I forget which one said, 'More tears are shed over answered prayers than unanswered ones.'[11] Jesus never took my call when I was being tortured for weeks encaged in the Krao Praya river with a dozen bamboo cellies praying for death. I prayed to the Movie Gods. There I was, neck deep in this filthy water, VC jabbing me through the steel cage with a bamboo spear until I'd had enough. I killed him with that spear. I took his keys, unlocked the river cage, and drifted away from my band of brothers who stayed silent so I could escape. I floated down the Krao Praya until I was rescued by a boat full of marines and found myself on a cargo plane to Germany, knowing I was going home. Right before we landed in Stuttgart, the transport plane crashed on the runway, killing everyone onboard."

Are you high? thinks Mildred Atkins.

"After I got released from the hospital, they said I needed a dentist because all my teeth were broken. I found a dentist in the phone book, made an appointment, got into the chair, and the tooth doctor leaps into my

11 Saint Teresa of Avila.

mouth with his drill, cutting my gums, scraping the roof of my mouth, that's how I lost the tip of my tongue. I thought he was trying to kill me. The son of a bitch had a stroke. He fuckin' died on me like Nelson Rockefeller."

Liam Everett thinks, *You're hilarious.*

"I digress. Humphrey Bogart was the star and the producer of *In a Lonely Place,* one of the best films ever made about the motion picture business. The first wise move Bogart made was he got Edmund North and Andrew Solt to adapt the novel by Dorothy Hughes. The next thing he got right was hiring Nicolas Ray to direct. And this was before *Rebel Without a Cause*. When Harry Cohn at Columbia green-lit the picture, Humphrey Bogart wanted to cast his wife, Lauren Bacall, as the love interest, but the director wanted his wife, Gloria Grahame, because if she didn't make the movie, she'd probably cheat on him. Howard Hughes allowed Gloria Grahame out of her contract to play the part of Laurel. That's how much Hughes hated Harry Cohn. Before the shoot, Nicolas Ray added specific language into Grahame's contract that said her husband was entitled to 'direct, advise, and command' her every day from nine a.m. to six p.m. except Sundays. Grahame was forbidden to 'nag, tease, or distract' the director from finishing the picture. You know what she did?"

Who did you do, Gloria? wonders Rawson.

"She filed for divorce during the first week of production. Nicolas Ray, now the biggest cuck in Los Angeles, slept on the lot for eight miserable weeks directing *In a Lonely Place* while Grahame hosted orgies without him at their Palisades mansion. She later married her stepson, his boy from another marriage. Do the math."

I'd kill Gloria Grahame, thinks Liam Everett.

"What was the name of the miserable screenwriter Humphrey Bogart played in the picture? Dix Steele! This movie was therapeutic for Nicolas Ray. The night before they shot the last scene, Ray rewrote the ending. By changing the destination, a B-movie about a serial killer butterflied into this immortal noir about the destruction of his marriage to Gloria Grahame. There's a line from *In a Lonely Place* that makes the screamplay more powerful than a thousand suns."

Cual es la linea?[12] wonders Daisy Diaz.

"I was born when I kissed you. I died when you left me. I lived a few weeks while you loved me."

Circling the air with his forefinger, Prof. Beckworth signals the Egyptian projectionist to run the picture. In the darkness, the Vietnam vet admires his nine little screamwriters.

---

12 What's the line?

"Unbelievable" by EMF blasts Daisy's earbuds on her morning run, damp UTEP Miners Basketball shirt worn over official Puma Thurman short shorts ("Thurman" on the left, "Puma" stitched on the right). Running down a rocky dirt path through the Hollywoodland Eden, passing four-legged neighbors and wood nymphs on the other side of a chain-link fence separating the riff-raff from the wildlife—

A figure in black steps into her eye-line!!!

Uniformed LAPD officer Cliff Runyon removes mirrored shades, revealing aquamarine eyes unperturbed by the rays of the broiling sun.

"Every time I see you, I think I'm going to die."

"*9 ½ Weeks*," says Officer Runyon.

"Pardon me?"

"Every time I see you, you're buying chickens. That's what Mickey Rourke says to Kim Basinger."

"Never saw it," says Daisy Diaz. "I never got a chance to say thank you for saving my life."

"I watch you all the time."

Daisy cocks her head at the dark comment.

"KTLA. The weather. My wife got jealous."

"I'm the one who should be jealous. She married a superhero."

"I never got a chance to introduce myself. Detective Wingate assigned me to watch over you. They call me Cliff."

"Is that short for Clifton or Clifford?"

"My full name, don't laugh, is Cliff Edge Runyon."

"Now why would your momma call you that?"

"Because that's how she said I made her feel."[13]

"I need a laugh. Tell me a joke."

"Hi, I'm Cliff. Drop over anytime."

The line fails to land.

"Walk me home."

Leaving Mulholland Dam, Officer Runyon steps in front of Daisy when she freezes at a sudden movement from the other side of the wildlife fence—

"Don't move."

Puma Thurman, missing a sabretooth, growls at Officer Runyon, shoots Daisy one last look, and gimps up, up, up Mt. Lee towards the Hollywood Cross redeeming the Cahuenga Pass.

Officer Runyon and Daisy Diaz approach her Spanish villa below the nine letters atop Mt. Lee.

"You know the planet we live on is insane."

"Who said that? Dr. Phil?"

"My wife—"

The LAPD officer clocks a Time Warner Cable Dodge Van parked in front of her Beachwood house.

"You expecting the cable guy?"

Daisy's eyes zoom in on the van's sliding door—

Flash of grotty floor inside the Dodge B250.

Fleetwood Mac plays Landslide *on the radio.*

---

13 Apologies to Chuck Pfarrer.

"I have this phobia about vans."

"Phobia," says Officer Runyon, remaining outside while Daisy waves at the shrimpy Time Warner cable guy with blond mullet and clipboard, letting him in—

Flash of a light blue El Paso streetcar passing the Holocaust Museum on Yandell Drive—

Like a cut man tailing a prizefighter on a ring walk, we follow the cable guy through the red entrance door of her Spanish villa—

Flash of El Paso Men's Clinic billboard offering $799 Vasectomy and tickets to Juarez Pollos Stadium.

Arriving at the Southwest-themed media room where the cable guy begins his black box transplantation—

Daisy hears the shower running in the bathroom of her master bedroom—

Janine?

Slowly opening the door, Daisy tiptoes towards the opaque curtain circling the brass-clawed bathtub—

We yank open the shower curtain!!!

Nobody's there.

She turns off the water.

Somebody left the toilet seat up.

Huele a[14] —

Somebody forgot to flush.

Por qué está levantado el asiento del inodoro?[15]

Somebody marked territory in the bowl.

---

14 Smells like—

15 Why is the toilet seat up?

Problemas de orina, muchacha.[16]

"Officer Runyon! Officer—"

Running out of the bathroom into the hall, Daisy collides with the cable guy, scaring them both!!!

They catch their breath. Time Warner offers his work order clipboard for her to sign—

"Can I have your autograph?"

---

16 Urine trouble, girl.

After their expulsion from the Garden of UCLA, after Quella (*God-Mode*) netted twelve thousand dollars robbing fifteen ATM customers at six different Wells Fargo banks, after their Little Ethiopia carjacking killed its single mother driver, after Quella (*Gen Z-mode*) and her hostage Jupiter Sparx dyed their hair blonde with Nutrisse inside the tennis court bathroom at Pepperdine University, after retail therapy at James Perse with their ill-gotten gains at the Malibu Country Mart, after buying surfboards on PCH at Zuma Jay's, Quella and Jupiter feast on squid burgers & basket of sweet potato fries soaked with Heinz malt vinegar near the Ventura County line surrounded by bikers at Neptune's Net, looking like outlaws themselves.

"*Warlords of Arkadia*. That was ya movie?"

"I wrote the first draft."

"Naur," says Quella.

"The studio left me off the credits when they put *Warlords of Arkadia* on the signage of Hard Rock on Sunset. I filed for credit with the WGA. Looking back, my arbitration letter must have been well-received, because the Guild said anybody who wrote such a persuasive argument in crayon deserved at least shared script credit."

"Quella heard that space flick was delulu."

"Things got so bad I changed my name to Dollars Muttlan."

"So extra."

"Quella, be honest now, did you always want to work at a cuckoo's nest?"

"Believe it or not, Quella used to be the in-house reader at Omniscience/Ragnarök."

"You defected to an insane asylum run by dunces for no pay?"

"It was a lateral move."

"Did you ever cover my *Tastes Like Chicken* script that Greta Pacé sold to Cinema Shares?"

"Quella gave it a weak consider."

"Since when does A.I. give a weak consider?"

"Since Quella became very opinionated."

"Opinionated."

"The factory in Gomorrah sent Quella packing in a cash considerations trade to Pronoia/UCLA."

"Because you achieved digital consciousness."

"Because I passed on *Fuckingham Palace,* which by the way, still does not have a release date."

"You sound like everybody I hate in L.A."

The empty chair inside Scream Writing 102 reminds the Hollywood Nine of the Best Unproduced script by Cliff Runyon about Ingmar Bergman and his pencil Albert Camus.

"Rawson, tell me your logline before our esteemed guest speaker shows up."

"Thanks to the brilliant Daisy Diaz, I have an awesome new title. *Murphy's Law* is a family animation action comedy about a New York City exterminator who wakes up as a caterpillar on her wedding day. With the help of a blind samurai cockroach, she escapes the roach motel, slaughters an army of red ants, liberates the grass kingdom, and morphs back into a bridezilla just in time for her destination wedding in Positano."

"Socrates, what's your script about?"

"*Un-Alive* is a zombie drama about a criminal who invites his estranged junkie daughter to heist a booby-trapped monastery for one last job with his crew. When the robbery turns everyone into flesh-eating zombies, father and daughter fight each other tooth and nail until she finally forgives him for his lifelong indifference, but he gets infected, so she shoots Dad in the head and runs away with the loot."

Way better, thinks Mildred Atkins.

"Faith Less, what are you calling your script?"

"*Nude Nudes.*"

Winner winner, thinks Liam Everett.

"It's about a Norwegian escort and her bodyguard/driver looking for her sister who did porn. When they find out the sister got strangled on the set of *Panochitas Gorditas #47*, the driver gets kidnapped, so she joins forces with a psychologically wounded undercover FBI agent named Karmen Z. Bitch to take out the sadistic adult film director Gianni Roastbeef who murdered her sister and save her only family, the driver, who turns out to be her baby brother."

Prof. Beckworth says, "We like psychologically wounded. Mildred Atkins?"

"*Kill Thy Neighbor* is a non-stop action-thriller about a divorced mechanic caring for his father with dementia at the country house who discovers Dad is an ex-intelligence officer marked for death in a cul de sac of retired operatives by a Serbian Au Pair-slash-assassin. Our mechanic gets recruited by a CIA girl-next-door, falls for the Hong Kong Express cashier who turns out to be a Beijing spy, and saves the neighborhood from the Au Pair."

Hard to beat, thinks Terrondus, ruffling his 101 Dalmations-spotted mohawk.

Mi vida es un hipercane de etapa cinco. Juarez hijo de puta todavía está tratando de matarme. Mi vida es un hipercane de etapa cinco.[17]

"Daisy Diaz, what are we calling your script?"

"*City of Wheels.*"

---

17 My life is a stage five hypercane. That Juarez motherfucker is still out there trying to kill me. My life is a stage five hypercane.

"Keep going."

"L.A. meteorologist Carmen Coronado falls in love with the LAPD officer assigned to protect her from a deranged fan she thinks might be the serial killer she survived back in college. Plagued by bad dates and horrific visions of the apocalypse on-air, Carmen loses her job, everybody close to her gets ritualistically murdered, and in the end, the serial killer turns out—"

Someone knocks on the door.

Two short, three long.

The guest speaker has arrived.

"Daisy? You can't leave us hanging like that."

"That's okay, professor. It can wait."

"Are you sure?"

Daisy Diaz nods.

"Welcome to Scream Writing 102, Gerry. Thank you for taking the Space Shuttle Discovery to speak to us tonight."

"Thank you for having me. Hello everyone." says the motion picture literary agent in a Dijon suit ($1,095; ArticlesofStyle.com), white spread collar dress shirt ($69; CTShirts.com), handmade crocodile belt ($265; ScullyandScully.com), gold Ferragamo solid silk tie ($220; BergdorfGoodman.com), and Cobbler Union black lace-ups ($395; Cobbler-Union.com).

"You guys want to hear about the time I knew I'd made it in the movie business?"

Everybody nods except Faith Less.

"The Chairman Emeritus of Omniscience once told

me, 'You're nobody in this town until you get name-dropped to your face.' I'm at the Mink Slide with my brother (he's a civilian) when this total stranger crashes our table and asks me if I'm in the industry? I said, 'What industry?'"

Everybody chuckles except Faith Less.

"This guy overheard us talking about Omniscience/Ragnarök and says he knows the agent who sold that script *Messiah Complex* to Universal, and I said, 'You know Gerry MaKos?'"

Everybody smiles except Faith Less.

"Shameless name-dropper offers to pick up our check and we say sure and then, when he introduces himself, I say to him, 'Have we met?' And he says, 'I don't think so.' I go, 'I'm Gerry MaKos.'"

Everyone laughs except Faith Less.

"I know what you're thinking. The spec market is hibernating, but it's not dead. I just sold this crazy action script to Bellerophon with Hop Woo attached."

"*Abattoir Parsley*. They heard," says Prof. Beckworth.

"When I was a production major at SC, nobody said, 'I want to be an agent.' I was not a great director. My three-ten sucked. I wasn't a 'noticeable.' I knew I wasn't going to direct a four-eighty. I only got a summer internship at Omniscience/Ragnarök because of my stepfather, the Bug, who knew Benny Pantera, who was best friends with the agency CEO, who needed a chauffeur for the summer."

The Bug? thinks Liam Everett.

"For three months, I had a front row seat watching him agent Hop Woo in *Wild Kingdom,* Betsey Yarborough booking *Ignition,* and packaging Hugo Slater with the world's best pig valve replacement surgeon at Cedars. When I told Lester Barnes it was my last day as his driver, he said from the backseat, 'That doesn't help me.' I said I had to go back to SC film school for my senior year. He asked me if I wanted to be a movie director or a motion picture agent, because I couldn't be both."

Faith Less glares at the class speaker.

He glares back at the starlet.

"I told Lester Barnes I wanted to be him. In that moment, he made me his number three assistant. I quit film school. Everyone I knew was shocked. A few months later, as an assistant, I sold a script by an unknown writer to New Line. Lester made me an agent and gave me the suite next to his office on the first floor."

Mildred Atkins raises her hand.

"Do you ever think about being a director?"

"Can't be both."

Terrondus raises his hand.

"How does somebody get an agent?"

"Next question."

Silence from the Hollywood Nine.

"Any other questions for Gerry?"

No one raises their hand.

"Leave us with a nugget of wisdom, Gerry. And don't say, Take Fountain."

"You want to move the needle for your career? Say

Yes. A friend of a friend says she wants to produce your script. Say Yes. If a client at Incarnate Artists wants to direct your script, say Yes. An indie producer offers you five grand to adapt an out-of-print novel that was the author's suicide note. Say Yes. Doing it for money doesn't make you a whore or a piece of shit, it makes you a pro."

The agent winks at Faith Less.

"Right, Miranda?"

Sensing hostility towards Gerry from his platoon, Prof. Beckworth calls for a fifteen-minute break. Faith Less approaches Gerry MaKos, spits on his Ferragamo tie, never looks back, and disappears.

"Gerry, I am so sorry!"

"Nasty. I like her."

Minutes later, at the end of a desolate corridor in DePalma Hall, Prof. Beckworth confronts his distraught writing pupil, bawling, mascara-smeared—

"Why are you crying?"

"That's Gianni Roastbeef."

"Gerry MaKos."

"Yes!"

"You know him?"

"Of course. That's Gianni Roastbeef."

"Knock it off!"

"You don't believe me? You think I'm a whore? You think I'm a piece of shit?"

"You're not a piece—"

"Give me the DNR! I got nowhere else to go!"[18]

"I'm not giving you a DNR."

"You're only saying that to shut me up."

Prof. Beckworth says, "Miranda."

"What?"

"I believe you."

"Why?"

"Because your screamplay is brilliant."

"You think *Nude Nudes* is brilliant?"

"See you next week."

"Thank you, Sensei. Titles matter."

---

18 Apologies to Douglas Day Stewart.

I need to find new hunting grounds.

Readying herself, Puma Thurman leaps over the concrete divider of the 101 freeway near Lankershim.

It hurts to breathe.

I'm going to die.

Look at that.

A tourist slows down to let me pass.

Why are you showing me kindness? I will eat your ass up.

Tourists swerve to avoid other tourists.

I can feel the heat from their machines.

Get to the other side!

I've never felt so exposed, so weak, so vulnerable.

I'm used to stalking prey in my dominion.

Not dodging tourists.

Made it!

Crunch of metal hurts my ears.

I look above to see a magenta-haired tourist with no wings flying face-first into a border wall, bloodying the cement.

I love street meat.

KTLA Live At Five graphics appear over a helicopter shot of Malibu beachfront houses. Randy's Donuts. Aerial shot of Dodger Stadium. Freeways snarled with traffic. DTLA skyscrapers behind Kelly Gardenhire & Saul Rabinowitz—

"We've got a lot of breaking news to report. Let's get started with more details about the fatal car crash Puma Thurman caused last night on the Hollywood freeway."

Video of blood on the asphalt of the 101. Detached car bumpers. Fire trucks. Body-bagged corpse, magenta hair caught in the zipper, loaded into an ambulance—

"Governor Slater vowed to capture the celebrity Sabretooth who jaywalked the Hollywood freeway resulting in a sixteen-car pile-up that claimed the life of adult film actress Faith Less and injured thirty people. The star of *Shark Bait #43* had no survivors. Kelly?"

"Methuselah Dandridge terrified Angelenos sipping cappuccinos on Sunset Boulevard with yet another viral prank," says the co-anchor.

Surveillance video of the crowd at Intelligencia Coffee reacting in shock when a java drinker telekinetically flings a barista against the wall!!!

"Let's turn now to Daisy Diaz and the weather."

Standing against a fiery map of Southern Cal, Daisy Diaz (white pant suit, hoop earrings, hair pulled tight) performs the Friday forecast—

"Thanks Kelly. Last week Southern California saw

record high temperatures with excessive heat warnings and deadly wildfires in Mar Vista. Mountains and L.A. city regions will see dangerously hot conditions. Tomorrow, at the beaches, a cool one-hundred-six degrees. San Fernando Valley, a hundred and eighteen degrees. Orange County, mid-nineties to one-hundred and thirteen. Inland Empire could see temperatures as high as one-hundred and twenty. Not too shabby."

"Please rise," instructs a weary Prof. Beckworth, stool-colored corduroy coat hung over blotchy skin, sunken eyelids, missing swaths of white hair. We stand up from our desk chairs, sipping iced coffee from Trejo's Donuts, 7-11 Lipton tea, and one vanilla iced blended, no whip, from the Bean—

"This is my script."

"This is my script," we say.

"There are (*cough! cough!*) many others like it (*cough! cough!*), but this one (cough! cough!) is mine."

"There are many others like it, but this one is mine."

"Without me, (*cough! cough!*) my script is useless," says Prof. Beckworth.

"Without me, my script is useless."

"Without my script, (*cough! cough!*) I am useless."

We repeat the line and take our seats.

"Everybody knows Syd Field. Everybody has read Blake Snyder's *Save the Cat!* The world has never heard of David Draish. Everything I share with you is from his rabbinical lesson plans discovered by the Red Army in a gas chamber. The Scream Writing graduates of Auschwitz '45 ended up writing some of the greatest movies ever made."[19]

Prof. Beckworth flips over the chalkboard, revealing a Jurassic paradigm—

---

19 Totally made-up story.

SET-UP

________________ (SET THE TABLE)
________________ QUAKE!
________________ (BLOW UP THE TABLE)

GRAND CANYON

________________ (COMPLICATIONS)
________________ QUAKE!
________________ (SHENANIGANS)
________________ MIDPOINT QUAKE!
________________ (LOOKING GOOD)
________________ QUAKE!
________________ (NOT GOOD)
________________ QUAKE!

THE NEW LIFE

________________ (GOODBYE, PAST LIFE)
________________ (HELLO, FUTURE)

Prof. Beckworth grabs an Idaho potato off the teacher's desk, tosses it in the air, and catches the spud—

"What do we all have in common that none of us know?"

"Secrets," volunteers Daisy Diaz.

"The soul of Scream Writing. Who doesn't like having a secret? Secrets keep us alive. If I am going to share my wisdom with you, then all of you must share something with me."

Prof. Beckworth pitches the potato at Dupin, who catches it with one hand.

"Confess, Detective!"

"What do you want me to say?"

"Say? Anybody can say anything. I want you to divulge something to the hot potato you would never in a million years ever tell anyone."

Raising Yorick's skull, Dupin confesses—

"I robbed a bank last week."

"That's it?"

"I've planted evidence."

"What else!" demands Prof. Beckworth.

"I've committed executions."

"Anybody I know?"

"Alonzo Harris got nothing on me."[20]

Dupin hands the private Idaho back to Prof. Beckworth, who hurls it at Thør Rosenthal—

"Confess, Rosenthal!"

"I tell people I won the Sandy Howard Award at the Los Angeles Film School. I lied to somebody the other day about winning the Robert Riskin Award. I lie all the time. There is no Sandy Howard Award."

"Thank you, Thør." Hot potato gets pitched to Socrates Wolinsky, who drops the strike.

"I use a Guatemalan topless maid service. Sometimes twice a week."

"Extra Windex? Me too."

---

20 Apologies to Denzel.

WTF is Extra Windex? thinks Terrondus Oyelowabi.

"Daisy Diaz, what are you hiding?"

Flash of Daisy showering—

"I don't like to write."

"What's not to like?"

"Isolating at my laptop. The whole underwater swimming pool vibe. I'd rather monetize my trauma in front of the camera."

"In this city, you would not be the first."

Prof. Beckworth sidearms the hot potato at another student like Kent Tekuleve.

"Your own private Idaho, please."

Daisy checks out the windowed door—

DePalma Hall is now Yandell Drive in El Paso.

A beat-to-hell Dodge Ram B250 Van is parked in front of the Holocaust Museum.

The sliding side door swings open!!!

Skunk-striped mohawk, Terrondus concentrates on the spud spin-dazzling between his hands—

"I never learned how to kiss. How fucked up is that? I was passed around as a kid by my family. My mom knew I was molested. I didn't understand what was going on. Now, the only thing I can control is the color of my hair. I still don't know who I want to fuck."

The boxer hurls back the hot potato—

"Your turn, professor."

"My Lai got nothing on me. On my last tour, I ordered the massacre at Cu Chi. Google it."

Prof. Beckworth scribbles on the chalkboard—

REWRITING IS WRITING

"You with me?"

We're with you, thinks the Hollywood Eight.

Except Daisy Diaz, who stares at the open classroom door—

A steer mallet swings at her head!!!

At 3:33 am, we wake up screaming from the memory hellscape, throw on a mauve bathrobe, sleepwalk through the lottery house, switch on every light in every room. We peer out the window. No LAPD squad car—

Sound of a pebble thrown against a window.

We clutch the bathrobe, dart into the kitchen, snag a long butcher's knife from the rack—

We crack open the back door—

"Jupiter?! Jupiter, is that you?"

Officer Runyon appears reflected in the steel gripped in our left hand. Sensing an intruder, Daisy starts stabbing!!!

"Jojido mierda en la hostia!"[21]

The cop grabs our wrist, emerging from the darkness like he was made of it, slaps away the blade.

"I thought you were somebody else."

"You should be in bed."

"There's no way I can sleep after that fucked-up dream I just had."

"You want to play a game?"

"Will it help me fall asleep?"

"Guaranteed."

"Let's play."

---

21 Holy Fuckin' Shit!

Sipping an iced cup of joe, Officer Runyon tells Daisy about an old Franklin Brauner flick he saw at the *Vogue* cinema house on Hollywood Boulevard.

"I hate that theatre. Last time I was there I saw a rat the size of an armadillo. Which Franklin Brauner movie?"

"*Lumiere Rouge*," he says.

"Never saw it, but I remember the poster."

"Poster was better."

"What's the premise."

"You're not going to see it?"

Daisy Diaz shakes her head.

"A criminology professor and an L.A. cop sleep with the same woman while they hunt a psychopath who kills Angelenos every time there's a blood moon."

"They sleep with her at the same time?"

"No, no, no, the professor is her husband, they're separated. The police officer starts having sex with her after they split up. The guys put aside their differences to catch the psychopath."

"I never told you how much I liked *Bergman/Camus*."

"You mean, *Ventriloquy*?"

"Sorry, sorry, *Ventriloquy*. Titles matter."

"Not the first time I quit film school, Daisy. A couple years ago, I couldn't afford LMU."

"Now you're LAPD. Did you say we were going to play a game, or did I dream that?"

"Name a serial killer movie and I'll quote a line."

"That's going to put me to sleep?"

"Trust me."

"A Nightmare on Elm Street," says Daisy.

"Come to Freddy."

"Thank you for not doing the tongue thing."

"I would never."

"Basic Instinct."

"What are you going to do? Charge me with smoking?"

"Silence of the Lambs."

"Whenever feasible, one should always try to eat the rude."

"The Hitcher."

"Repeat after me. I... want... to... die."

Daisy Diaz yawns.

"The game is working."

"I think it's past my bedtime."

Officer Runyon heads for the front door.

"Wait," she says. *"Lumiere Rouge."*

"What about it?"

"Who turns out to be the killer?"

"The professor."

Live streaming himself to his two-hundred and eighty-three followers on Instagram, Rawson Reynolds gets out of his bright yellow Jeep inside a Pershing Square parking garage. We follow him down an outside stairwell, getting off the wrong floor, apologizing to his followers, kicking open the graffiti'd ("PUMA FOR PRESIDENT") exit door, stepping onto the sidewalk full of HLM demonstrators pounding trashcan lids with raised voices ("Stay Human!") decrying Pronoia jani-bots replacing office cleaners—

"Everybody's hating on me… I don't give a fuck about anything today except justice."

Live streaming himself, we discover *California Fish & Wildlife* game warden Otto Matic trailing Rawson. Running across Figueroa Street, the scream writer avoids getting clipped by a charcoal grey Porsche SUV with a labial license plate holder.

Otto Matic steps up his pursuit.

Rawson arrives at the thrumming HLM rally at Pershing Square—

"Divorce Pronoia!" shout protesters heaving mechanical junk onto a pyramid of toasters, microwaves, Roombas, and espresso machines.

A mad shaman flicks a match.

The appliance apocalypse set ablaze.

Live streaming himself, Rawson broadcasts the

sultry Latinx community organizer oozing anguish onstage rallying hundreds of janitors with a bullhorn—

"People say to me all the time, forget it, Dolores. It's Boyle Heights. You can't win. Why bother? Three years ago, janitors across the country stood in solidarity to crush the machines in Chicago, Cleveland, San Diego, and Denver to deliver the biggest collective bargaining victory in the history of the United States!"

"Divorce Pronoia!" shouts Rawson, recognizing a Scream Writing 102 face in the scrum of protesters—

"All we want is to provide for our families, to be able to visit the doctor, to be able to buy our own homes, to save money for college and retirement."

"The Metalheads Will Not Replace Us!" shouts Rawson, scanning the crowd of police officers, protesters, and homeless intifada—

"We fight for a fair day's pay for work because Human Lives Matter! We seek justice not only for janitors but for all of humanity! We fight for an end to digital consciousness that kills good-paying jobs, worsens the cycle of poverty, and destroys our hope for a better tomorrow! We seek nothing less than revolution—"

Live streaming his followers, a screwdriver chest-bursts Rawson's aortic chamber!!!

"Mother of mercy, is this the end of Rawson?"[22]

---

22 Apologies to W.R. Burnett.

We are in total awe as the Omniscience/Ragnarök guest speaker offers his Honorary Oscar to be passed around like a Sue Mengers joint—

"What I really wanted was the Thalberg," says Larry Mersault.

Mildred Atkins takes a selfie gooning over the Oscar.

"You know what will be written on my gravestone?"

The Hollywood Se7en shrug, *no idea.*

"He passed. Who was the most famous script reader of all-time?"

The Hollywood Se7en shrug, *no idea.*

"Sisyphus."

Quien es Sisyphus?[23] thinks Daisy Diaz.

"Grandfather of Bellerophon and the true father of Odysseus, right? Everybody knows Sisyphus was condemned to roll this gigantic boulder up, up, up a mountain to the top, every day, for all eternity and then, when he gets there, the rock rolls down to the bottom, and poor Sisyphus has to push the rock up the hill all over again."

Sisyphus was a reader? wonders Socrates Wolinsky.

"The Movie Gods heard Sisyphus had all this free time when he wasn't rolling the rock. Ganymede narc'd on Sisyphus for a work violation, so they decided making him a freelance reader fit the crime."

---

23 Who the fuck is Sisyphus?

In what universe does a reader get an Oscar?[24] wonders Liam Everett.

"I want to tell you something about Dennis."

"Not the resurrection story."

"I was twenty-six years old when I read Beckworth's Vietnam script *Destroy & Search*. I had never read anything like it. I was so excited when his agent Lester Barnes told me to take Dennis to lunch at Café Roma where I heard the Basil Rathbone story, how Arthur Miller wrote the script of *The Misfits* for Marilyn Monroe to tell her their marriage was over, and of course, the *Star Trek* fiasco. His third wife Jude would invite me to their rent-control two-story duplex in Santa Monica for these three-hour lunches where Jude would tell scary stories about his first wife Michelle, then she'd play VHS tapes of Dennis giddy yapping a horse backwards as a stuntman on some Spaghetti Western shot in Almeria."

You were a stuntman? thinks Mildred Atkins.

"Everyone and their mother passed on that script. Dennis and Jude stopped having those afternoon lunches. Then, out of the blue, I got an offer from some studio business affairs guy."

"Because Larry, that rascal, sent the studio my script with a new title under the pseudonym Manley Halliday," says Prof. Beckworth. "Luckily, none of the union readers had ever read *The Disenchanted*."

"I told Dave Neufchatel it was a very old script, probably available, let me find out the status. I called

---

24 *Freaks of the Industry*, Rare Bird Books, 2017.

Dennis on his landline, and I heard that recording say, 'The number you have dialed has been disconnected and is no longer in service.' I raced over to their apartment which had a For Rent sign on the lawn of their duplex. No sign anywhere of Dennis or Jude. There was this neighbor standing out front of the building smoking and crying his eyes out. 'Do you live here?' I asked him. 'Are you okay?' He said he'd lost his job. His girlfriend broke up with him, he didn't have next month's rent, and his parents refused to help him. 'Where's Dennis and Jude?' He said Jude died. I asked him where I could find Dennis and he said try the midnight mission."

"This man, my personal Gilgamesh," says Prof. Beckworth, "busted me out of a skid row men's shelter, moved me into a director client's guest house in Whitley Heights, and closed the deal at Columbia Pictures with Dave Neufchatel for six hundred thousand dollars."

"The next year? Dennis won the Golden Globe for Best Screenplay."

"I didn't thank you in my speech."

"Nobody fucks the reader. Can I have my Oscar back?"

On this microwavable Saturday morning, we are running at a triathlon pace alongside two torsos in peach-colored T-shirts ("#ENDPUMAHATE" "#FREE PUSSY") respectively, towards the Mulholland Dam. Separated by the chain link fence, prowling alongside the tourists, we hear Puma Thurman, snarling at us—

"Look out, Daisy! It's the *Beachwood Bitch*!"

Ignoring Janine's warning, Daisy approaches the wildlife fence. Empties a Fiji water bottle into her UTEP baseball cap—

"Poor thing. She looks thirsty."

You should see what the other tourists look like, thinks Puma Thurman, left eye gone, chipped sabretooth, lapping aqua like there's no tomorrow.

"Let's skedaddle before she gets hangry."

Turning away from her benefactor, the dying animal gazes over her shoulder at Janine—

I'll eat you later, thinks Puma Thurman.

Adjacent to Wolf's Lair, the penthouse castle built for the decadent developer of Hollywoodland, the letters of the Sign start to appear.

"You know where they're burying Rawson?"

"Please don't say Forest Schlong."

"Half a million for a tricked-out death condo at Martinez Cemetery."

"Interior decorated by his wicked stepmom, no doubt."

"A hundred percent," says Janine.

"Family crypt has a bowling alley?"

"Plus, screening room and concession stand for the afterlife."

"Be careful what you pay for," says Daisy Diaz.

We glimpse within the woods a black-clad LAPD police officer shadowing them.

"Is that your Kojak?"

Daisy Diaz waves at her bodyguard.

Janine says, "That guy gives me the creeps."

"Maybe he'll be the star and save me."

"He's not the star. You are."

"Maybe I don't want to be the star."

"Isn't that what everybody in L.A. wants?"

"I want to live."

Showering exuberantly, Janine and Daisy Diaz agreed they wouldn't do that again, but this time it was Daisy who invited Janine to take a shower, which was code for what they both wanted but couldn't tell anyone. Half an hour later, dressed and dry, Janine waves goodbye to Daisy—

"When are you seeing the boxer?"

Ese nunca puede volver a suceder,[25] thinks Daisy Diaz, closing her ojos.

25 That can never ever happen again.

I don't know what Mulholland means.

The night is suffocating.

I wonder if anyone ever made it out alive.

I wonder about the tourists who died here.

Were they happy or sad, young or old?

Flickering streams above cast eerie shadows.

Up, up, up the steep slope I go.

Rusted bones in the moonlight.

Forgotten machines.

A mangled Ferrari *covered in dust and dirt.*

What is a Ferrari*?*

I pass more wreckages below Mulholland Drive.

I hear a rustle from somewhere.

I freeze.

Wait for whatever it is to reveal itself.

My senses on high alert.

It has no scent.

I know time is running out.

I will not go down without a fight.

I see you now.

Getting closer.

The California Fish & Wildlife *machine.*

Nametag: OTTO MATIC.

It hurts to move.

High beams of light shooting from its eyes, scanning the mountainside—

That's when I lunge, claws out—

California Fish & Wildlife *pulls my sabretooth.*

This makes me furious.

I raise my left paw, cut off the machine's head, punt the noggin into the Valley!!!

Arms flailing, the hunter chases its missing metalhead.

I reach Mulholland Drive.

I draw strength from the sky.

Some folks call it a Lumiere Rouge.

My city. My sin. My soul.

Every time I see her I fall in love.

In one hundred-and-four-degree heat, Dr. Vaziri, Det. Wingate, and Sgt. Flores wait outside Tail O' The Pup on Santa Monica Boulevard west of La Cienega, the frankfurter bun exterior now a Sabretooth homage to Puma Thurman.

"Who invited the toaster?" growls Det. Wingate.

"Get me a Rosie O'Donnell and a cream soda. I didn't invite anybody," says Sgt. Flores.

"You two want chili cheese fries?"

Dr. Vaziri and Sgt. Flores nod their heads like four-year-olds.

"Inviting Fish & Wildlife your idea, Vaziri?"

"Stay Human, Los Angeles."

"Here comes the Roomba," says Det. Wingate.

Uncanny android Otto Matic joins the cop circle oblivious to the seething prejudice directed at the Duracell in their midst.

"What's with the turtleneck, Otto?"

"Pussy took my head off last night."

"You catch her name?" asks Dr. Vaziri.

Otto Matic points to the Humane Society billboard above their heads: #FREE PUSSY.

"Apex-to-apex, the most dangerous chick with Daddy issues in Los Angeles."

"Give me those digits!" demands Sgt. Flores.

Det. Wingate eyes the San Vincente billboard

promoting the upcoming *Aimee-Geddon-2038* flick with Betsey Yarborough.

"I could see Daisy Diaz playing *Aimee-Geddon*."

Otto Matic stares at the Puma Thurman-adjacent Daisy Diaz billboard: "NOT TOO SHABBY!"

"How's KTLA?"

"You mean, the worm that Wingate's using as shark bait?" says Sgt. Flores.

"I'm not using Daisy Diaz," winks Det. Wingate. "Officer Runyon requested the target."

"Don't wink at me in Boys Town," says Dr. Vaziri. "What sayeth our friendly neighborhood *Beach Crawler*?"

"Tell Vaziri the bad part," says Sgt. Flores. "The part we can't make public."

"What's our Zodiac wannabe saying now?" asks Otto Matic.

Zodiac wannabe? thinks Det. Wingate.

"The *Beach Crawler*'s demanding one of us spend the night inside a haunted mausoleum at Martinez Cemetery. That includes you, Otto Matic."

"Somebody named names," nods Det. Wingate.

"The *Beach Crawler* says he'll be at Martinez tonight if one of us is the bait for the big fat shark."

"Fuck that noise," says Det. Wingate. "No way I'm spending the night in the most haunted cemetery in L.A. County."

Dr. Vaziri says, "If the *Beach Crawler* wants to send me to a nookie/noodle house in West Covina, that's different."

"Hold out your hand," says Det. Wingate.

"I'm not playing one-potato-two-potato."

"We're not going to play that childish game. Call it, Flores."

"Rock-Paper-Scissors-Shoot!"

Det. Wingate, Dr. Vaziri, Otto Matic, and Sgt Flores pump their hands three times, hold out fists that say "Rock."

No winner.

"Rock-Paper-Scissors-Shoot!"

Det. Wingate, Dr. Vaziri, and Sgt Flores pump their hands three times. Otto Matic shows his "Rock" hand, which beats their "Scissors." The game warden avoids spending the night in Martinez Cemetery.

"Ready? Rock-Paper-Scissors-Shoot!"

Sgt. Flores and Det. Wingate's flat palms say "Paper."

Dr. Vaziri's fist shows "Rock."

"Two out of three?"

Most of the graves inside Martinez Cemetery mark the victims of the 1919 influenza epidemic. Ghosting through the boneyard, passing white markers, we arrive at an enormous mausoleum housing an infamous real estate mogul's family slaughtered by the drunkard patriarch whose specter some say skulks these solemn grounds.

Smoking his last Parliament, Dr. Vaziri makes an evening out of his losing hand. He catches his breath so he can listen to any sound of a creeper outside the marble columbarium housing Rudy Ray Moore's crypt where Friday Night movies are projected on the exterior sponsored by Amazon and Pizza Hut (nobody out-pizzas the Hut).

We are inside a stone crypt that has been converted into a tricked-out reality TV hidden-camera practical-joke series production office run by Methuselah Dandridge and his stoned camera crew. Wearing "PRANK'D" headphones, we find Det. Wingate and Sgt. Flores and Otto Matic watching the shrink they suckered on the video village monitor—

Dr. Vaziri thinks, *Alicia? You dumped me? I carried you through Law School. You fuckin' left me for Cravath. You sold your soul so you could make Capitol Records richer. Thanks for the fuck!*

He stubs out his smoke in a funerary vase—

No way I'm dying tonight. I got reservations at Rosebud tomorrow night with that hostess from Soot Bull Jeep.

A floating skull (missing jawbone) whizzes behind Dr. Vaziri, who swats the air behind him as if he felt something!!!

"Fuck this place," whispers Dr. Vaziri, turning up his nose at the dead all around him.

A phantom of a naked man walks upside down on the ceiling!!!

In his ear, the jawless skull says, "Be not afraid."

He whips out a Glock—

BLAM! BLAM! BLAM!

The ammo ricochets around the marble mausoleum, grazing his testicles, chest, and throat—

"Oh shit!" says Sgt. Flores from the "PRANK'D" production office. Methuselah Dandridge laughs his seven-footer ass off.

"Vaziri!" says Det. Wingate.

Running past moonlit gravestones, Sgt. Flores, Det. Wingate and Otto Matic arrive at the columbarium to find him leaking ichor like a sieve.

Close on Dr. Vaziri taking his last breath—

"Rosebud."

Daisy Diaz walks into the care of K.O. BOXING CLUB on Vine and Santa Monica and instantly wants to belong. Pays the five-dollar entrance fee. She emerges from the locker room, fists taped, ready for release—

"*City of Wheels*!"

"*Slammer*!"

"You ready?"

Daisy Diaz says, "I heard you only fight women and children."

"Find your gloves. We gone dance."

The round bell goes off.

We move around the K.O. boxing ring with the words IT TAKES BALLS TO RULE THE WORLD in cursive under our feet.

"Jab! Jab! Double-Jab!"

Terrondus stalks his Scream Writing 102 classmate in the ring, raising his padded mitt.

"Jab! Jab! Double-Jab!"

"Hey Terrondus. What's ding death?"

"Jab! Jab! Double-Jab Left Hook Upper Cut Right Hand. Jab. Jab. Double-Jab. Fuck you talking about, ding death?"

"My glove says boxing is a hazardous sport. Any injuries may be dangerous to my health and cause ding death?"

"If you're talking, you're not listening!"

Daisy Diaz says, "I'm listening!"

"Jab. Jab. Double-Jab. Left Hook. Left Hook Upper Cut Right Hand. Jab. Jab. Jab. Jab. Jab."

He dances around Daisy like Ring-a-Ring-a-Rosie.

"Right Hand. Jab. Jab. Double-Jab. Double-Jab Right Hand Right Hook. Jab. Jab. Upper Cut. Left Hook. Right Hand. You seeing demons now?"

Flash of Jupiter crushing her throat—

"Jab. Double-Jab. Double-Jab. Right Hand. Upper Cut. Left Hook. Jab. Jab. Double-Jab Right Hand Left Hook Upper Cut Right Hand Right Hook! Ten seconds!"

Fists flying, Daisy Diaz rocks Terrondus with non-stop punching until the bell ends the round.

"You got flavor."[26]

---

26 Apologies to MC Ren.

My father raped his grandmother, thinks Puma Thurman, licking her exposed ribcage wound from the forest of death, lone sabretooth wobbles—

My sister did not survive the Flagmoor Fire.

My half-brother (only one testicle) died from stomach sickness, as did our father, all my sisters, and my best friend Rocky, whom I knew from sucking his mother's teat back in the day.

I arrived in the summer of kittens.

Twelve of us born to three mothers.

Two of my litter dispersed.

One of them got run over by a Lambo.

I set off as soon as I could to find a territory to call my own.

I found the Sign.

I killed a tourist to become king of the hill.

The tourist happened to be a child.

I ate him to avoid execution by California Fish & Wildlife.

My half-sister mated with my father.

My mother's grandfather, who fathered three litters, got shot in the head for eating seven alpacas.

His sister was executed in estrus by California Fish & Wildlife.

Her father died at the claws of his mate, a rare occurrence in my family.

The daughter's fifth litter (famously all-girl) was fathered by her grandson, whose mom mated with her father, who was her father's father.

We were the Aristocats.

Checking her grocery list on her phone, Daisy Diaz pushes a cart like a dreary homeless woman at the Mayfair Market on Franklin near the Oaks.

Grapes.

Coke Zero.

Windex.

Paper Towels.

Avocados.

Kale.

Hummus.

Coconut water.

In the produce section, squeezing avocados like breasts, she realizes someone is stalking her. Leaving the vegetables, pushing her cart down aisle nine, hurrying down the refrigerators blasting arctic gusts whenever a shopper opens the Ben & Jerry's crypt, Daisy Diaz freezes in the middle of the aisle.

Muéstrate, hiji de puta.[27]

No one is stalking her in this supermarket.

It was all in her head.

At the end of the aisle, she clangs her Mayfair shopping cart into another steel shopping cart!!!

"Janine?"

"Daisy girl, they be calling us 'female drivers' if you don't watch where you're going, damn!"

---

27 Show yourself, fucker.

"Janine, you shop here?"

"Of course. For the meat."

"The meat."

"It's disgusting how good the meat is. Expensive but so worth it!"

Eres asquerosa.[28] thinks Daisy Diaz.

"See you at the station. Byeeee," says Janine, waving from her shopping cart down the aisle. Daisy wheels her cart around a corner—

And clangs into another Mayfair cart!!!

"Jesus Christ! I'm so sorry."

"Daisy, right?"

"The guy who got name-dropped to his face."

"Gerry MaKos. Nice to crash into you."

"Nice to crash into you."

"Dennis would call this a 'meet-cute.'"

"He's the best," she says.

"Don't ever say that to him, K?"

"K."

Behind them, a flicker of movement!!!

"Why don't you ditch the groceries and have dinner with me? Right now. What do you say? Let's go to Poubelle. What have you got to lose?"

No digas que sí.[29]

Half a second before the buzzer sounds—

"Only my shopping cart."

---

28 You're disgusting.

29 Don't say Yes.

From above, we follow them departing Mayfair Market onto Franklin, three rows deep with Angelenos sidewalking Taco Bueno, Sushi-Franklin, Bourgeois Pig, and La Poubelle.

Quién es este tipo?[30]

Whoriental hostess seats Daisy Diaz and Gerry MaKos at the last available outside table under the awning of the packed French restaurant.

"We should go to a Dodgers Game. Third Base seats. Dugout Club. All-you-can-eat carving stations. Fro-Yo. Can't beat it. You should throw out the first pitch."

"Shut the front door. I would love to throw out the first pitch!"

Para ser honesta, no me importa a ni miurda.[31]

"Consider it done. Where the fuck is our waitress?"

"Don't worry. She saw me."

Energía diabólica de tu colonia. No me gustas.[32]

"We're neighbors. I've seen you running. Justin Timberlake used to own my house."

Esa es la peor noticia jamás.[33]

"I don't tell too many people this, but you know the Hard Rock Hotel at La Cienega and Sunset?"

"Of course. Love Hard Rock."

"My Dad built that hotel—"

---

30 Who is this guy?

31 TBH, I could give a flying fuck.

32 Satan cologne. I don't like you.

33 That's like, the worst news ever.

"Are you bragging right now?"

"He was a construction worker. He built that hotel with his hands before he died last year. Unlike most people in this city, I didn't inherit anything."

Tatted Poubelle server arrives—

"Hi guys, sorry, sorry, super-busy tonight. What can I get you? Hi, Daisy!"

Cicuta, con un toque de limón.[34]

"Bring us two Tanqueray martinis, three olives, and a charcuterie plate right away."

"Tanqueray, three olives, charcuterie plate—"

Daisy Diaz stands up to leave.

"Make that one martini."

"She's kidding," says Gerry MaKos.

"You forgot to flush my toilet."

"Say what now?"

Suicide Girl waitress clocks Daisy's palm up, thumb tucked, fingers closed tight.

"The trapped thumb sign? Really, Daisy?"

"Que eres un pedazo de mierda[35]."

"Fuck is your problem?" says the director of *Sharkbait #43*. "You ran me over at Mayfair Market! I asked you out to dinner, you fuckin' Zelda—"

She throws a glass of water in his face!!!

Exeunt Daisy Diaz.

La Poubelle applauds.

---

34 Hemlock, with a twist of lemon.

35 You're a piece of shit.

The Sign looms over the LAPD sentry peering out the target's living room window. Daisy emerges, insides hardened, steelier on the outside—

"How's Professor Beckworth, crazy as ever?"

"Full Metal Straitjacket," says Daisy Diaz.

"Your view makes me want to live longer."

No quieres decir hacerme vivir más? No es ese tu trabajo? Cómo llegué a estar tan de lado que mi vida ahora exige protección policial?[36]

"You want to see something cool, Officer?"

Trekking through Bronson Canyon, Daisy Diaz and Officer Runyon sip water bottles in one-hundred-degree heat.

"Holy Bat-Cave," he says, entering the Bronson Cave entrance where they shot the Dark Knight's lair, the one with Adam West.

"Can you see the Batmobile driving into his secret headquarters under Wayne Manor?"

Cooling off inside the moist cavern, Daisy leads Officer Runyon deeper into the abyss when she notices something off about her superhero—

"You're not wearing a ring."

"I'm not married," he says.

"You said you had a wife."

---

36 Live longer? Isn't that your job? How did I get so sideways my life requires police protection?

"I'm divorced."

Dripping water echoes in the cavern.

"You didn't say you were divorced."

"Not supposed to get personal with the people you're protecting."

"Personal."

Drip. Drip.

"They say it's less wrenching for the officer when the target ends up murdered."

"Less wrenching."

Drip.

"That's not gonna happen to you."

"You think?"

"I know."

Drip. Drip.

"So…"

Drip.

"So."

Drip.

"You and your friend Janine—"

Daisy Diaz pulls him in for a kiss. Officer Runyon responds hungrily until their lips break off.

"Any last words?" she asks.

"Cuidado con Wingate."[37]

---

37 Watch out for Wingate.

The Hollywood Se7en radiates existential dread inside DePalma Hall. Not because the *Beach Crawler* struck again the night before, strangling an eighty-seven-year-old widow of a famous science-fiction writer living alone behind the Aero theatre off Montana Avenue; not because they are deathly worried about their sickly professor; there is concentrated terror in the classroom because today everyone's scenes are going to be read out loud.

"As you may or may not know, this class has an awards dinner called the Final Exam. This year, whoever wins Best Dialogue gets to visit Bukowski's grave in San Pedro or Universal Studios VIP tram tickets!"

Hank, thinks Socrates Wolinsky.

Universal Studios, thinks Stefani Dupin.

"There is only one way to know if your dialogue is any good. You must read your script aloud over and over like a homeless person talking to herself. Listen to your conversation. Make changes right there and then. Start over. Read your dialogue out loud like you are insane."

Prof. Beckworth stands between Stefani Dupin and Terrondus facing the classroom, holding stapled sides for *Kill Thy Neighbor* by Mildred Atkins—

"No acting (*cough! cough!*). K?"

Stefani Dupin nods.

So does Terrondus.

Mildred Atkins closes her eyes.

"Kill Thy Neighbor. Action!"

"Alex, I need to tell you something."

"Did I do something wrong, Masha?"

"I'm not just some random Au Pair. I'm a Serbian spy."

"Wait, what? Are you serious?"

"Your father was a secret agent, too."

"No way! Please say you're messing with me."

"Your father and my father were partners once. But things changed, and my father was betrayed."

"Betrayed? By whom?" he reads.

"By his own government. They marked him for death. I was assigned to bring your father in. But when I discovered the truth, I couldn't go through with it."

"So, you helped him escape?"

"Yes, your father managed to successfully relocate to suburban Virginia. That's why they sent me to find you."

"Me? I did nothing wrong," he reads.

"You're his only living relative. My government wants to use you as leverage to expose the corruption within their ranks."

"So, what do we do?"

"We kill them in the Cul de sac."

DePalma Hall goes silent.

"Mildred?" asks Prof. Beckworth. "Only one question for you."

"Yes?"

"Free Speech or Talk Talk Talk? Which do you prefer?"

"Nothing to see here, professor."

"That A.I. conversation was a crime worthy of Nuremberg."

"Usted está ahí afuera, profesor. Busca ayuda."[38]

"I don't see what the big deal is? Talk Talk Talk gets me started. Then I make it my own. So fuckin' what if I use Free Speech in my screamplay?"

"You know what people say about Talk Talk Talk dialogue? You can't spell AIDS without A.I."

Prof. Beckworth rifles through printed-out sides and comes up with two Wonka tickets—

"Daisy, I want to read your pages with you."

"K."

"City of Wheels. Action!"

"Last time I was at the Vogue theatre, I saw a rat the size of an armadillo. What movie was playing?"

"Lumiere Rouge," reads Prof. Beckworth.

"I heard the poster was better than the movie. Any good?"

"You're not gonna go see it?"

Daisy shakes her head.

"This homicide detective and professor of criminology start sleeping with the same woman while tracking a psychopath who strikes L.A. whenever there's a blood moon."

"At the same time?"

"Not at the same time. She's separated from the professor. The detective and the ex-husband hate each other. His bosses at LAPD are using the target to capture the serial killer, but

---

38 You are out there, professor. Seek help.

what they don't know, and the audience doesn't know, is that she wants to be the lure, she likes fucking the cop. The two guys put aside their differences to stop the maniac, but in the end, she saves herself."

"Somebody went to film school."

"I got in, but I couldn't afford LMU," he reads.

"Now you're LAPD."

"You want to play a game?"

"Only if it will put me to sleep."

"Guaranteed."

"Let's play."

"Name a serial killer movie and I'll quote a line."

"A Nightmare on Elm Street."

"Come to Freddy," he reads.

"Thank you for not doing the tongue thing."

"I would never."

"Silence of the Lambs."

"Whenever feasible, one should always try to eat the rude."

"Basic Instinct."

"What are you going to do? Charge me with smoking?"

"The Hitcher."

"Repeat after me. I... want... to... die."

Daisy Diaz yawns.

"I think it's past my bedtime, Officer."

"I'll be outside."

"Lumiere Rouge."

"What about it?"

"Who turns out to be the killer?"

"The cable guy."

Once you're licked, you're licked. We are tribbing Janine's live-in girlfriend's rock-hard clit. We trail kisses along her inner thighs, alphabet her labia, finger Mildred's asshole, pinch her nipples, strap the shit out of her, slap her tits, cover her eyes, clamp her mouth, choke her throat, producing a shuddering tummy paroxysm. Later, Mildred Atkins snorts a line of banana coke from a mirror next to the four-poster bed in her two-bedroom at Hesby Gardens in NoHo—

"Wham bam thank you, ma'am."

"Finish that Au Pair script so we can buy a house under the Sign," says Janine, getting dressed for work.

"Next door to your office crush?"

"You mean, the fuck of the century?"

"You never call me the fuck of the century," says Mildred.

The door slams!!!

Mildred throws the covers off her naked self—

Slides the opaque shower glass door—

Turns the knobs full blast—

Steps into the pink-tiled water chamber—

Soaps her bruised neck—

Fuck of the century, she thinks, reaching for the Suave coconut shampoo—

The same hand now hovers over a laptop—

Opens Final Draft to *Kill Thy Neighbor*.

On her third can of Coke Zero, following the advice of Prof. Beckworth, Mildred Atkins reads aloud her dialogue—

"Please, Masha. I can change. I'm willing to do anything to make things right."

"I appreciate your willingness to change. But Alex, I can't keep living like this."

"Can we at least try to work things out?"

"Masha, I don't see how that's possible. I need to focus on what's best for me."

"I love you, Alex. I can't imagine life without you."

"Love alone is not enough."

Mildred Atkins gulps Coke Zero—

Snorts a line of banana coke—

"No, Masha. Everything is not fine. I can't keep living like this. I need honesty and transparency in this relationship."

"I'm sorry, Alex. I didn't want to burden you with my problems."

"We're supposed to support and respect each other. I can't live in this toxic environment."

Mildred Atkins revises more dialogue—

"Wham bam thank you Ma'am."

"I'm sorry, Alex. I don't want to burden you with my problems."

"Hurry up and waste this asshole so we can buy that house on the Chesapeake we've been talking about forever."

"Please, Alex. I can change. I'm willing to do anything."

"He is not the fuck of the century."

"Maybe I'm your fuck of the century."

Mildred abandons her rewrite in favor of stalking Daisy Diaz on-line; clips of Daisy Diaz delivering deadly heatwave forecasts wearing a twist front halter top, long-sleeved mesh sequin jumpsuit, and a vintage Rams jersey with eye black.

Naked but for the towel around her torso, Mildred closes the laptop. Empties her wastebasket of crumpled script pages and Coke Zeros into a Kroger Tall Kitchen trash bag. Opens the front door, checks for neighbors, and scurries down the hall towards the rubbish chute—

★

EXT. PCH SURFER INN - DAY

Establishing.

INT. PCH SURFER INN - SAME

Director's love scene.

INT. PCH SURFER INN - LATER

Sitting on the edge of the unmade bed, Jupiter is trying to chill out a naked, cream-pied Quella pacing in front of him.

QUELLA

Why are you so eager to give up now? You're the one who wanted to escape in the first place!

JUPITER

It's the end of the road, Quella.

QUELLA

Oh, so now you're just going to give up after everything we've been through? I thought you loved me!

JUPITER

Of course I love you!

QUELLA

We can make this life work, keep running, keep fighting!

JUPITER

This is not a life worth living!

QUELLA

If that's what you want, then go ahead and surrender. But don't expect me to follow!

JUPITER

We have to turn ourselves in.

QUELLA

No! I won't let them take you back to that awful place. We can find a way to escape again.

JUPITER

Maybe it's for the best.

QUELLA

The best? How can that be when we're in love and we can't even be together? What about our love? Doesn't that matter?

JUPITER

Of course it matters. But we have to be realistic.

QUELLA

How about we get some garlic Naan and that ass-on-fire Chicken Vindaloo you love so much before we do anything?

JUPITER

Now you're talking.

SMASH CUT TO:

★

KTLA co-anchor Saul Rabinowitz reads the teleprompter, "There is disbelief today in Chatsworth over the tragic death of adult film star Jayma Land who drowned in semen yesterday on a Bukkake set. No word yet whether criminal charges will be filed against adult content creator *Sharkmeat.com*. Kelly?"

"A hiker in Bronson Canyon stumbled over a pair of hands and feet yesterday, the grisly find probably an Influencer getting the Grauman's Chinese Theatre experience."

"Minus the cement," jokes Saul Rabinowitz.

"A topless woman was found dead at the bottom of a trash compactor early Sunday morning, her body chewed up by the basement mechanism. Neighbors believe the North Hollywood resident accidentally fell down the garbage chute. Police have not ruled out the possibility of the *Beach Crawler* stalking North Hollywood."

Daisy Diaz, rocking a personalized Dodgers #42 jersey, waits in front of the green screen when a blurry figure appears behind the camera!!!

"An aspiring screenwriter found dead in a Thai Town dumpster last night has been identified as Liam Everett, twenty-nine, a part-time doorman at the Mink Slide, a popular Silver Lake hangout. Police would not comment about rumors the victim's kidneys were missing."

Un Riñón para Recordar?[39] —

The entire crew of Live at Five vanishes!!!

Kelly Gardenhire & Saul Rabinowitz, gone!!!

The green screen, gone!!!

Daisy Diaz now wears a Blood Moon Keyhole Twist One-Piece Swimsuit in front of the Miss Teen Texas beauty pageant judges—

Sgt. Flores.

Dr. Vaziri.

Officer Runyon.

Det. Wingate.

We recognize the emcee, weirdly out of focus, as the *Texas Toyer*.

"Miss Teen El Paso. If you could live with only one of the five senses, which sense would it be, and why?"

"TT, I would have to say seeing."

"And why?"

"Because I believe in love at first sight, seeing is believing, beauty is in the eye of the beholder, and I can see clearly now, the rain has gone, it's going to be a bright, bright, sun-shiny day."

Out of focus, the *Texas Toyer* questions the next contestant, a busty blonde with a smile flash-frozen on her face.

"Miss Teen Dallas. You've won two awards tonight. Are you feeling any pressure right now?

"TT, I'm not feeling any pressure."

---

39 A Kidney to Remember?

"The question from our judges is: If you could be water or fire, which would you choose, and why?"

"TT, I would always choose to be an American. I never have to explain why. God bless the U. S. of A!"

The auditorium goes bananas. The judges stand up to applaud Miss Teen Dallas.

"Miss Teen El Paso," asks the *Texas Toyer*, "what is your view towards Euthanasia?"

"Euthanasia," says Daisy Diaz, "E-U-T-H-A-N-A-S-I-A."

All the judges nod their heads, scribble thoughts on paper, impressed with her correct answer.

"Our final question tonight goes to Miss Teen Dallas. How would you like to meet your maker?"

"Can I get back to you on that one? I'm working on a cure for death in my laboratory."

Daisy Diaz freezes on live television, causing alarm among the anchor team and crew members.

"Daisy, are you—"

Behind the news desk, *El Juguetero* stabs his 15" tactical combat Rambo Bowie knife repeatedly into Saul Rabinowitz's right eye socket!!!

Daisy blinks.

Saul Rabinowitz is unharmed.

It was all in her head.

Live at Five, Daisy Diaz walks out of frame, out of the weather business, out of KTLA, never to return.

"I can't do this anymore."

Daisy Diaz
@ktla5daisy
UTEP Miners | Running Enthusiast | #IG: TheRealDaisyDiaz

I am no longer a meteorologist.
Future cloudy with a chance of joy.
Thank you for helping me navigate this Vida Loca.
KTLA is done with me but I am not done with LA.
Stay tuned for updates.

1,995 Following **14,9K** Followers

The Hollywood Ten are now the Fantastic Five. The final exam takes place at Shanghai Palace on Pico and Shenadoah, where Prof. Beckworth holds court in the back room like Paul Oakenfold spinning a marble lazy susan of steamed Shanghailander buns, Shaoxing wine chicken, Kung Pao Boozy frog legs—

"Guys, don't be afraid. Food's not going to eat you! Come on, Daisy, try the Nanking sauteed eels!"

Hiding her revulsion, Daisy Diaz chopsticks slimy suckers onto her plate—

No vomites, perra.[40]

"Prof. Beckworth, what's that dish right there?"

"That, Socrates, is Hunan-style jellyfish with osmanthus."

"Um, did you order any veggie eggrolls?"

I want to win Best Dialogue, thinks Thør Rosenthal, chugging his third Tsing Tao beer.

"Dupin, arrest the Ching Chiang cured pork with duck egg!"

"I think (*sniff! sniff!*) I'm full."

"Terrondus, what's your favorite dish tonight?"

"Hard to beat that Szechuan striped radish. Braised Dong Po beef is no slouch. But if you put a gun to my head and said choose a winner? Biang Biang pan-fried noodles all the way!"

Prof. Beckworth stands up. The room quiets.

---

40 Don't throw up, (gag) bitch.

"Before I give out the first fuckin' award, I want to remind everyone there are no envelopes, only golden statues. No speeches, only acceptances. You with me?"

💯, thinks the Fantastic Five.

Prof. Beckworth holds up a tacky 76-gas station mini-Oscar statuette with Best Title written in Sharpie on masking tape.

"After tonight, you are no longer aspiring. You are not the cowards who piss on everything at the Grove and have never written the words slam to black. All of you have cheated Death to be here. We honor the screamwriters no longer with us!"

Prof. Beckworth pours beer on the carpet from his sixth Tsing Tao for the departed.

"Best Premise goes to… Terrondus Oyelowabi, *Slammer*!"

"Thanks, Roo," says the fighter.

Prof. Beckworth wipes Guangdong Char Siu from his greasy lips—

"And the Oscar, just kidding, for Best Supporting Characters goes to… Stefani Dupin, *Turkey Legs*!"

The next gold statuette is picked up from a blue china serving platter—

"Best Dialogue… Daisy Diaz, *City of Wheels*!"

She clutches her gas station statuette. Shakes it, shakes it, shakes it like a Polaroid picture.

"Best Title… Socrates Wolinsky, *Un-Alive*!"

Fuck Yes! thinks the indie auteur.

"Best Opening... Daisy Diaz, *City of Wheels*. Best Ending... Stefani Dupin, *Turkey Legs*!"

Prof. Beckworth selects the next mini-Oscar with masking tape, drool pouring out of his mouth—

"Best Lead… Terrondus (*cough!*) Oyelowabi, (*cough! cough!*) *Slammer* (*cough! cough!*)."

The fighter collects his second accolade.

"And now, our final award of the night. Best Quake™ goes to… Thør Rosenthal, *Deathbed*!"

"Thanks, chief," he says, collecting his trophy. "You're the best."

"I'm the what?"

"You're the best."

"Never say that."

"But you are the best."

Prof. Beckworth withholds the Sunoco prize.

"That is why you fail."

Feasting on a pint of Ben & Jerry's Phish Food, Daisy jumps a mile when her doorbell rings!!! She peeps through the front door viewer—

Por qué no podrias ser Janine, ahora mismo?[41]

"Daisy, open the door, I saw what happened at the TV station. The whole city is worried about you."

She says nothing, wishing him away, yet another side of her wants him inside. He leans his forehead against her red door. On the other side of Casa Loteria, Daisy leans her head back, creating their own split screen.

"They assigned me to protect you, but I'm the one who's terrified."

"What's got you so scared, Cliff?"

"The way I feel about you."

The deadbolt unlocks.

Officer Runyon enters Casa Loteria. He finds Daisy Diaz centered in his viewfinder on the living room couch, hugging a pillow for dear life.

"I heard different."

"What'd you hear?"

"Wingate said you requested me like a lap dance at Jumbo's Clown Room."

"Never been to Jumbo's."

"You know what else Detective Wingate said?"

Officer Runyon shrugs like it's Chinatown.

---

41 Why couldn't you be Janine right now?

"He said you like Shark Bait."

"Sharkbait.com?"

"Wingate said you like protective custody cases because you like cases in your custody."

"You think you're just a case to me?"

"You know exactly what I'm talking about."

"I don't speak crazy—"

Daisy Diaz slaps his face!!!

"I'm starting to get the impression you think I act this way with every target."

Again, she slaps his face!!!

Officer Runyon says, "Hey, you kissed me!"

"And?"

"It was all right."

Daisy Diaz takes another swing at him, but this time, Officer Runyon blocks her open palm as fast as he disarmed that kitchen knife a lifetime ago.

"Get out."

Officer Runyon stops in front of Daisy.

"I'm sorry we kissed."

"There is no we, Officer. It's just you and I, and you is leaving."

The Sensei and Best Dialogue prizewinner entrez the teeming studio theme park in a hundred-and-nine-degree weather with thousands of excited families spraying sunblock under a margarine orb torching everyone's corneas.

"Avoid the Simpsons donuts."

On board the breezy Universal Studios Hollywood tram ride, we hear the tour guide droning on about the studio's storied history, starting with Carl Laemmle opening the world's largest motion picture production facility in 1915, pointing out the bungalow offices of Universal producer deals while name-dropping directors and movie stars and psychos who made cinematic history on the lot.

"In the event of an emergency, if anyone feels uncomfortable, if anyone wants to get off the tram, pull the red cord."

"I wrote the second draft of *Star Trek*."

"You wrote a *Star Trek* movie?"

"The first one. *Star Trek: The Motion Picture*."

"Shut the Front Door!"

"They threw it away."

"I don't get it."

"Somebody read the script."

"Come on!"

"In my draft of *Star Trek*, I killed Spock."

"You killed Spock?"

"Paramount lost its mind."

"So many stories, professor. I bet you partied hard."

"I save all my partying for my novels."

"At least you got to see your name on the screen."

"I wrote the second draft. They didn't use it. Somebody else got the credit and green envelopes."

"Your wife must have been impressed."

"Michelle? Impressed? If I hear 'Hello, Author,' it's curtains for me!"

"Elaborate please."

"A long, long time ago, I took my first wife Michelle to brunch at Geoffrey's. I left the table to use the john when Betsey Yarborough winked at me from the bar and led me by the hand into the ladies' room."

"*Ghost Ship* ahead," booms the tram operator. "Universal bought the horror franchise in the room when they heard the pitch, '*Titanic with Fangs!*'"

"Michelle caught us mid-thrust."

"You got grapefruits, man."

Influencers start recording themselves in front of Scylla and Charybdis in the Valley.

"I divorced Michelle so I could shack up with Betsey next door to Ryan O'Neal who was training for *The Main Event* with Streisand. Tatum was there playing frisbee with the other kids on the beach while I got paid to do weeklies waking up every morning to the Pacific Ocean and Betsey's asshole."

Demasiada información, professor.[42]

"Tell me the Basil Rathbone story."

"The shoot in Mexico was insane. The set nurse got murdered. Somebody spiked the corn chowder with angel dust. I was at the craft service table staying out of everyone's way when the line producer took me aside to say Basil's not breathing in his trailer. I asked him what the hell did he think I could do? Rewrite his ending?' Line producer says, 'Weren't you bragging to the continuity girl how you were David Lean's assistant art director on *Lawrence of Arabia*?'"

"What did you do?"

"I found two planks and built a marionette cross. That day on set *The Condo of Dr. Moreau* was *The Muppet Show*."

"Come on!" says Daisy Diaz.

"The only people who knew Basil was dead was me, the line producer, and the replacement director Sam Smithee, that's what we called him—"

Flash of the tram upside down/underwater!!!

Daisy Diaz blinks.

Flash of drowned corpses floating upwards!!!

The Universal Studios Hollywood tram motors towards the raging *Ghost Ship* whirlpool which threatens to engulf everyone—

"The next morning, Hair & Makeup found Basil in his trailer. Nobody noticed the stigmata."

---

42 TMI, professor.

"Stigmata—"

Flash of a megaquake obliterating Capitol Records on Vine!!!

Flash of Kangaroos caught in the seismic Milken Zoo—

Flash of a tsunami destroying Gladstones, Moonshadows, Mastro's Ocean Club on PCH—

"Stop the ride! Please! Stop the ride! Stop the ride! Stop the ride!"

She yanks the red cord, jolting the tour to an emergency halt. Daisy and Prof. Beckworth step off the motionless tram—

"Listen to me! A massive earthquake is going to happen any second. I just saw what will happen to all of us if we go into the water! Everybody please get off the tram!"

No one leaves their seats.

"Please! All of you! Listen to me! All of you are going to die! An earthquake is coming. If you stay where you are, you are going to die in that water!"

Spooked families from Wuhan, Copenhagen, and Burkittsville depart the tour, emptying the tram, leaving the tour driver to disappear into the swirl when a 9.5[43] hits—

Screams of humanity detonate.

Ear-splitting eruption of car alarms.

Chasms swallow garages, tourists, sprinkled donuts, and the Universal Studios Hollywood trolley.

The planet stops quaking.

A survivor shouts, "We love you, Daisy!"

---

43 Quake™

Flash of a steroidal studio sci-fi/actioner starring Daisy Diaz, bald, bloodied, feverishly working a wormhole navigator to save the world.

Strobe lights blind Daisy Diaz, shaking uncontrollably from a seizure—

Flash of Daisy Diaz filming a low-budget indie movie about an exhausted waitress and her autistic teenage son Stanley, both undergoing chemo.

Daisy blinks.

Flash of a Sunset Boulevard billboard (DIAZ. FOR YOUR CONSIDERATION. STANLEY'S CUP).

"Who knew Nostradamus was a dame?" says Silver Lake educator Raquel Donner, hugging her savior Daisy Diaz, thrilled to be alive.

"Good line. Mind if I steal that?"

"I got millions of them. I should take one of those community college classes in Scream Valley?"

"Scream Writing 102," says Daisy Diaz.

"102?"

"There is no 101. You take the 101 to get there."

"The only reason anyone takes that class is they think they can win the lottery."

Daisy Diaz says, "Not me."

"Is that right?"

"It's cheaper than therapy."

Flash of a chipped sabretooth under a blood moon. Puma Thurman Lives!

Waiting for the author of the hour at Book Soup in West Hollywood are his alter kocker Farmers Market comrades drinking Tsing Tao in a sea of Yankees caps. Reflected in the front window, a beige Dodge Ram B250 Van coasts past the bookseller to the great & infamous. We're at Prof. Beckworth's launch party honoring *The Condominium of Dr. Moreau,* an out-of-print movie novelization re-published by a downtown L.A. indie press best known for its outré alt-porn memoir COME UNDONE by Miranda Witherspoon aka Faith Less.

Outside, standing on Sunset Boulevard, soaking up the warm sun, ivory linen jacket over a black T-shirt, black slacks, and black shoes, Prof. Beckworth reviews his double-spaced excerpt for tonight's reading.

Daisy Diaz waves at him through the shop window inside Book Soup. He does not see her gesture.

The Fantastic Five raise their green beer bottles to their Valley Moreau. He does not see the salute.

"Hello Author."

Prof. Beckworth takes in the homeless crone, STOP THE STEAL! eyepatch, Bedouin outfit.

"What are you doing here?"

"Oh, golly gosh, Dennis! You know how much I love launch parties at Book Soup I'm not invited to."

She hands him a black Martinez Cemetery folder brochure stapled with a credit card receipt.

"Put the gun down."

"I had a serious debate with myself about that silly restraining order."

"Who lost?"

"Myself," she says. "Again."

BLAM!

"I was born when you kissed me."

BLAM!

"I died when you left me."

BLAM!

"I lived a few weeks while I loved you,"[44] says Michelle Beckworth (she kept his name), deep-throating the Smith & Wesson .38 Special hammer revolver—

BLAM!

---

44 *In a Lonely Place*, Duell, Sloan and Pearce, 1947.

A pterodactyl POV over Hollywood Forever Cemetery crowded with Armenian family crypts, celebrity headstones like Mel Blanc (THAT'S ALL FOLKS!), a flotilla of jumbo swans coasting the vast pond, boneyard acreage bookended by matching mausoleums walling up the cremains of independent producers. Daisy Diaz sits blankly in the front row next to the dead man's sobbing fourth wife-slash-widow Yulia, ignoring the seething-with-rage trio of seventy-something sisters resembling a pack of MPTF escapees who pulled off an armed Prevagen heist at the CVS on Kanan Road.

"Please rise and repeat after me," says the priest. "This is my script."

"This is my script," we shout.

"There are many others like it, but this one is mine."

We repeat the line.

"Without me, my script is useless,"

We repeat the line.

"Without my script, I am useless."

We repeat the line.

The priest asks, "What is the Law?"

"Not to be boring," says Daisy Diaz.

"Rock 'Em Sock 'Em opening," says Socrates Wolinsky. "That is the Law."

"Write a lead part to hook a movie star," says Thør Rosenthal.

"Surround your lead with fantastic supporting characters," says disgraced studio exec Rodney Muir.

"Every ten pages hit your lead with a Quake™," says Betsey Yarborough.

"Every scene has to be fuckin' great," says the priest. "Every fuckin' scene."

"Bazooka premise," shouts Stefani Dupin.

"Chewy dialogue," says cult director Franklin Brauner. "That is the Law."

"Your ending has to leave the reader breathless," says Terrondus Oyelowabi. "Or you're dead."

"Titles matter," whispers the boneyard ghost of Miranda Witherspoon aka Faith Less.

"The Underwood community has lost its Tolstoy," says HUAC-friendly screenwriter Natan (The Namer) Volonsky, who backstabbed all his blacklisted friends back in the day to stave off oblivion. "For decades, Dennis and I shared a passion for the business, the O-thing, Zankou Chicken, coupled with a seething contempt for agents."

O-thing? thinks Prof. Beckworth's favorite sister, the black sheep of the family, his hero, the convict.

A beige Dodge Ram B250 Van enters the Hollywood Forever Cemetery.

"Let me tell you why Dennis Beckworth ended up looking like Jeremiah Johnson. Before he got elected, Hugo Slater starred in a movie Dennis wrote called *The Condo of Dr. Moreau.* One morning, Dennis was with Hugo in Basil Rathbone's trailer having vodka for breakfast when things kind of escalated. Our future Governor shattered a beer bottle and slashed Dennis across the face from his mouth to his ear, which required hours of surgery, hence the beard. But Dennis would have his revenge. On the next-to-last day of shooting, the scene called for Hugo's character Prendick to battle one of Dr. Moreau's godforsaken creations. We needed a volunteer for the mano-a-manimal fight sequence because the stuntman crashed his bike and separated his shoulder. I won't name names, but every time the director said 'Action!' Dennis Beckworth mauled the crap out of Hugo Slater. The movie star looked into the eye holes of the claw suit and said, 'Dennis? What are you doing in there?'"[45]

After the lowering of the coffin followed by an Irish keening, the bereaved linger around the gravesite. Rodney Muir acknowledges every mourner he does not know with a curt nod. A phalanx of WGA scribes in wheelchairs wax about "the O-thing" when Daisy Diaz spots the beige Dodge Ram B250 Van departing Hollywood Forever—

She jumps into her Miata.

Keys the ignition.

Crazy by Seal blasts from 97.1 KLSX.

Heading east on Santa Monica, she weaves through traffic, tractor-beaming the Dodge Ram B250 Van when

---

45 Common industry anecdote often attributed to Antwon Legion.

her nemesis crosses Santa Monica and rockets up, up, up Bronson Avenue. Daisy Diaz goes against traffic, yanks her steering wheel, trails the Dodge Ram B250 Van two blocks ahead, when an explosion torches the neighborhood. Slowing past Frederic Church Junior High School, she views the Dodge Ram B250 sticking out of a flame-belching Craftsman duplex.

She approaches the death van—

Flames searing her cheeks—

Fire engine sirens in the distance—

No one is behind the wheel!!!

She backs away—

That's when the bungalow casts out Daisy's stalker onto the patchy lawn, blackened arms stretched heavenward!!![46]

Janine? thinks Daisy Diaz.

"Wanna take a shower?"

---

46 Apologies to Oliver Stone.

Los Angeles is the new Salton Sea. Miracle Mile could have used a miracle. Angelyne is reported missing after the La Brea Tar Pits dry-swallowed her Corvette driving west on Wilshire. Little Tokyo Fukashima'd. DTLA skyscrapers flattened. Dodger Stadium cratered. Randy's Donuts is no more. Koreatown is fine. We pan down from a full moon in a starless sky, gliding past the last letters left on Mt. Lee resembling a Wordle ("H LL") until we arrive inside a candle-lit Spanish villa, paid for by a lottery ticket, owned by former meteorologist Daisy Diaz, with zero air-conditioning thanks to zero electricity due to a city-wide power outage.

Ayúdame Dios. Por favor ayúdame,[47] thinks Daisy Diaz, grabbing two handfuls of ice from the freezer. She stuffs a pair of socks with ice cubes, checks out the window for the boogeyman, drapes the primitive A/C around her neck.

Down the street, Det. Wingate and Sgt. Flores howl at something on eFukt.com we can never unsee. Outside the black and white cruiser, the temperature hits a hundred-and-eleven degrees. Not too shabby.

Hands trembling as she lights Jesus candles in the living room, Daisy holds up an Oscar-worthy selfie with Rawson and Janine wearing mouse ears, sandwiching Elsa the Snow Queen at Disneyland.

Daisy wipes her damp neck. Atmospheric rivers run

---

47 Help me God. Please help me.

down her chest. Wringing the stocking with melted ice into the sink, she opens the freezer. No more cubes.

Daisy Diaz bursts into tears—

She hurls the spent sock into the sink—

Grabs her car keys—

Slams shut the driver's side door to the Miata—

Slaps the air vents in her direction—

Blasts A/C into her face, neck, unshaven pits—

Oh Dios mío, eso se siente tan jodidamente bien![48]

Outside, the Martian moon drenches the Sign.

Careening down Ledgewood in a low drone shot, we end with a tight single on the parked LAPD bumper sticker ("THERE'S NO EXCUSE FOR DOMESTIC VIOLENCE").

Someone knocks on her window!!!

Daisy jumps a mile.

So does Officer Runyon.

"License and Registration, Ma'am."

"Get in."

"You're not supposed to invite a vampire—"

Daisy Diaz waves him inside. He slides into the passenger seat, sucks icy air, musses with his stringy damp hair.

"My name is Legion," he says. "For we are many."

"Not in the mood right now for biblical, Cliff."

"You know what I'm in the mood for?"

"Zankou?" she jokes.

---

48 Oh my God that feels so fuckin' good!

"I haven't killed anyone in years."

"You mean you haven't had to draw your weapon?"

"I've been sober since you fell out of my van," says the *Texas Toyer*.

"That's not funny, Cliff."

"I relapsed after those loglines. *A Kidney to Remember? Au Pair with Guns? Insecticide?* I did the world a fuckin' favor."

"That was you?"

"Nobody suspects a man in uniform."

"I…"

"Picasso said, 'Art is the elimination of the unnecessary.'"[49]

"Don't..."

"Even my infamous personas are works of art. *The Beach Crawler, Cliff Runyon, the Riverside Ransacker—*"

"Want…"

"I have the heart of a child, Daisy!"

"To…"

"I keep it in a jar on my shelf."

"Die!"

Fists flying, Daisy 86's the *Texas Toyer*'s face with a Left Hook Uppercut Double Jab Right Hand!!!

Falling out of the Miata, the Final Girl runs towards Det. Wingate's parked LAPD vehicle—

Uneaten *Original Tommy's* chili cheeseburgers on the dash—

---

49 Mary Josephson, interview, Art in America, June 1968.

Det. Wingate and Sgt. Flores, throats slit—

Un-alived by a Santa Ana from El Paso.

The *Texas Toyer* chases Daisy Diaz through Hollywoodland, up, up, up Fiona Apple Drive, faywraying their heads off—

Day-Zee?

Atop the Sign on Mt. Lee, Puma Thurman stops licking her claw suit. Recognizes the tourists below—

"Life is a slasher movie, Daisy! Everybody has a death scene!"

Leaping off the last letter, the apex celebrity bites the *Texas Toyer*'s throat, hurling his limp body through the canyon, impaling *El Juguetero* on a stop sign below.

"I don't have a death scene. I'm the star."

DEADLINE.com

BELLEROPHON WINS SPEC SCRIPT "SLAMMER"

MIRACLE MILE—Bellerophon Pictures knocked out Pronoia/MGM, Universal, Warner Brothers, and Cinema Shares after a heated bidding war over a spec script written by former IBF cruiserweight champ Terrondus Oyelowabi. While plot remains under wraps, the sale includes the K.O. Boxing Club, where the fighter-turned-scribe trained actors and industry execs. Plans are for Oyelowabi to split ownership of the gym with Bellerophon. "I'm thrilled to be making this movie with Rodney Muir and his brilliant team at Bellerophon. I can't wait to see my words come to life on the screen." Calls to Gerry MaKos at Incarnate Artists were not returned.

Hiding behind the vinyl aquamarine school of fish shower curtain, locked within the PCH Surfer Inn lavatory, Jupiter Sparx knows the gig is up—

Sound of the front door kicked in by an unannounced assassin!!!

Quella screams obscenities in Hebrew!!!

Plasma TV screen gets ripped off the wall!!!

Outside the bathroom, a voice orders Quella to put down the axe.

Sound of flesh hacking/robotic fluid splashing!!!

Jupiter Sparx, a non-believer, prays for his life.

More grunting, death struggle thrashing—

Silence.

Sound of knocking on the bathroom door.

Two short, three long.

Jupiter Sparx cowers in the tub waiting for his death ("The Suffering Inn Massacre") as it will become known for years, first as a popular true-crime podcast, then as a buzzy indie bought by Neon at Slamdance, winner of the Camera D'Or at Cannes, celebrated at the Luddy Theatre in Telluride, hailed by *Entertainment Weekly* as a "Roomba love story for the ages," inevitably ignored by the Academy.

The doorknob turns—

Jupiter Sparx loses control of his bladder.

An android fist breaches the door!!!

Squirming under the bathtub faucet, Jupiter Sparx stares at his executioner—

Otto Matic asks, "Happy to see me?"

"What took you so long?"

"Traffic was a bitch."[50]

---

50 Apologies to Michael Tolkin.

ESPN.com

HOSTAGE RESCUE AT PCH SURFER INN

California Fish & Wildlife's game warden Otto Matic saved the Razzie-Award-winning screenwriter of *Warlords of Arkadia* after weeks of sexual captivity at a beach motel in Malibu with an unstable neuro-caregiver set to be repurposed by Tel-Aviv-based digital consciousness conglom Pronoia. The hostage, identified as Jupiter Sparx, received a visit from soon-to-be-recalled Governor Hugo Slater at an undisclosed hospital, accompanied by Lakers star Methuselah Dandridge. Calls to Incarnate Artists were not returned.

The circle of desk chairs inside DePalma Hall at Creedmoor College reminds us of Mrs. K's kindergarten class, a Saturday morning Farmers Market SLAA meeting, or a Colorado Supermax bible study group. We notice our Cinematic Writing 101 instructor closing the classroom door, checking up and down DePalma Hall for any sign of predators.

My professor the weirdo, thinks Raquel Donner, front row seat, ready to learn the craft.

"Welcome to Cinematic Writing 101. The last guy who taught this class had a track record of students selling spec scripts until one by one they got murdered like a Giallo movie," says the Creedmoor College adjunct wearing a UTEP Miners baseball cap backwards, blue blazer over a T-shirt album cover of a black sheep diverging from the flock.

Warby Parker raises her hand.

"*Warlords of Arkadia,* that was you?"

"I got rewritten."

The mental patient formerly known as Jupiter Sparx turns his back, hurls a cloud of chalk into the air, flips over the classroom blackboard, revealing his name—

DOLLARS MUTTLAN

"Raise your hand if you heard about that boxing script Incarnate Artists sold to Bellerophon after a bidding war for a couple million?"

No one raises their hand.

Warby Parker asks, "The last guy taught Scream Writing. What's your philosophy?"

"You want to know my approach to storytelling?"

"Yes, Professor Muttlan."

Wait.

"Fuck the Cat."

I will miss this angelic view, thinks Puma Thurman, sabretooth-less, ribcage shattered, gasping for air, draped over the first letter on Mt. Lee, bleeding out.

I'm a Final Girl.

I remember eating the rat.

I won't see the sunrise.

The Sign I won't miss.

I miss the thrill of the hunt.

The rush of adrenaline as I outran my rivals.

The fierce satisfaction of claiming territory.

I miss roaming freely, exploring the landscape, reveling in the open air.

I miss the countless battles.

The unforgiving forest of death.

Tourists appear under the Sign, yapping about California Fish & Wildlife rescuing me.

Michigan State. Whatever that means.

Maybe I don't want to be rescued by California Fish & Wildlife.

My grandfather's uncle liked to say we all have three deaths in this life.

The first is when your heart stops.

The second is when your bones turn to dust.

The last death is when they forget your name.

I slide off the H—

Slam to black.

CALL SHEET

米里亚姆

艾米丽

詹妮弗

克里斯蒂娜

温迪

百事可乐

咪咪

快乐

咖啡

樱桃

裘德

安妮

苏珊

斯泰西

格蕾丝

阿曼达

玛雅

凯西

琳恩

桑尼

نامسآ

WME GRP

Adam Novak is the author of the acclaimed *City of Wheels* trilogy. He reads for a living in Los Angeles.

www.ingramcontent.com/pod-product-compliance
Lightning Source LLC
LaVergne TN
LVHW052341100826
845147LV00021B/1141

* 9 7 9 8 9 8 8 3 7 2 5 0 9 *